SHAWNA MICHELLE

Timeless Temptation

An erotic drama

By Shawna Michelle

About the Author

Shawna Michelle is a hardworking and motivated, wife, mother and working professional, who has always had a passion for writing. She's been writing poetry and short stories since she was a teenager, her first self-published book was Swipe A Real Online Entanglement, an erotic novel. Timeless Temptation is her second self-published novel. Shawna Michelle enjoys writing about unspoken sexual fantasies and forbidden pleasures, combined with entertaining drama.

She lives in the metro Atlanta area with her husband and young sons. She's an evolving woman who encourages people to live without fear of judgement and do what they love. Throughout her life she's lived behind the shadow of managing depression and the anxieties created by the opinions of others. Writing continues to be both liberating and detoxifying. Writing is her medication for anxiety and stress, and it allows her to explore parts of herself that would otherwise remain hidden.

About the Book

Timeless Temptation is an erotic drama about a young girl, Londyn Banks, who through her naïve and lustful fantasies wants to lose her virginity to her father's colleague Victor Crawford, who's almost twice her age and married. After several purposeful encounters with Victor, she sees her opportunity to fulfill her fantasy with him. Careful not to interfere with her dreams of graduating she engages in a secret sexual romance with him. However, time and life's progressions separate them, only for them to find their way back together, twenty years later, after her father dies. Suddenly she is forced to navigate the complexities of love and loss, leading her to an unexpected relationship and career. A shocking revelation emerges, challenging her resilience in ways she never anticipated.

Dedication

Dedicated to my friend Andriene Patricia Walker, born December 30, 1983 and last seen on September 8, 2003. It's been twenty years since anyone has seen her, but we haven't forgotten about her. Andriene was my elementary school best friend. We were the tallest in the class and more mature for the third grade. We were the pretty, smart, tomboys in the school. She came from a big Jamaican family where they all lived together and prayed together. I envied her big family and I loved spending the weekends at her house. We'd be down in the basement of her house, watching music videos or the ABC network TGIF TV show lineup on Friday nights or SNICK on Nickelodeon on Saturday nights. Other times we'd be in her room lost in our own world of playing with our Barbies, playing Super Nintendo, reading Sweet Valley High books or riding our bikes around the neighborhood with the rest of the neighborhood kids. From a young age we knew our bodies were different and we got the boys attention playfully. But we both had major body insecurities, her insecurities stemming from her vitiligo throughout her body including her face, her hands and her legs. And my flaws, well you name it and I found the flaw in it. I thought her flaws were uniquely beautiful. I remember when we had to take swim lessons and she wore pants to cover her skin due to the discoloration on her legs and she felt embarrassed. So, the next time we had swim lessons I wore my black ballet tights with my bathing suit so she wouldn't feel alone or embarrassed. She always had my back, and she was like a big sister to me, she didn't let anybody mess with me at school or around the neighborhood.

She was a really great dancer and a singer, we often listened to TLC, SWV and Whitney Houston together on her boombox. I on the other hand struggled with dancing and although she tried to teach me how to dance in front of the mirror, the only dancing I could do was two step. She was my best friend and we were inseparable until the fifth grade. That's when my family moved to Florida and I couldn't be with my best friend anymore. I wrote her letters over the years and ran up my parents long distance phone bill talking to her on the phone. Every time my family would go back to Philly to visit I would go to the old neighborhood to see her. We kept in contact throughout the years until the last time I saw her during the summer of 2001, as we were entering our senior year of high school. We met up for pizza at a familiar spot that we used to hang out in. Although she was still beautiful and funny, she didn't seem like the Andriene I once knew. She shared some things with me that concerned me, but I was so happy to see her I ignored all the signs that something was wrong. Then life kicked in for me with graduation, a boyfriend, working a part-time job, caring for my family and traveling, I let time slip away. Years passed and I hadn't heard from her and I assumed she was ok somewhere living her life, like me and that one day we would catch up on lost time. Until, one day as I was preparing for the birth of my son, I saw one of her family members online and I sent him a message and asked if he had heard from Andriene. I wanted to share with her that I was expecting soon. I wondered if she had children of her own. That's when he explained that no one had seen or heard from Andriene in years. I couldn't believe what I was reading. I was so mad at myself for not remaining in contact with her over the years. I was mad at myself for taking her and time for granted. She was a beautiful, intelligent and courageous young woman, who deserved so much more than this world gave her. Andriene was that friend that forced me to love myself despite my flaws and I'm forever grateful for her.

She taught me a big lesson about life with her absence. She taught me to love on the people you care about and let them know how they make you feel and don't let "The Stuff" get in the way.

Love You Angie!

Timeless Temptation

An erotic drama

CHAPTER ONE

The familiar sounds of SWV's harmonic song, Weak, filled the air from the Bluetooth speaker as I sat on the porch of my lonely home, sipping a glass of red wine. A gentle breeze swept through my graying hair, carrying with it the sweet scent of blooming roses. The sun's warm rays kissed my glowing skin, casting a soft glow over my face. I inhaled the sweet floral scent in the air, triggering my mind to wander back to a time long ago, to the memories of my first love.

My mind wandered to a time when life was filled with endless possibilities and the thrill of youth. I was a fun, spirited young girl, my heart untouched by the world's complexities. And then, like a wisp of enchantment, he walked into my life.

Every once in a while I would think of him and daydream about what I would do if I ever saw him again. That beautiful chocolate brown man, that made my young, curiously pure pussy wet at the thought of him. At any moment in my life I could close my eyes and see his obnoxiously white teeth against the soft creases of his full lips creating his captivating smile and the angled perfection of his lightly salted goatee. I got caught up in the moment, lost in the memory of how I felt when he looked down at me, gazing into my tempting naïve eyes, from his six-foot frame. I hadn't heard that man's voice in twenty years. I wondered if I would still recognize him if I ever saw him again. Or, if the resonating sound of his baritone voice that once sent chills down my spine would ever do it again. Or, if I would ever have my thighs wrapped around his back again. Could time change him to become unrecognizable to me, I questioned? I would daydream about the times we were together and what he meant to me as a young teenage girl. I dreamed vividly and in color and when I closed my eyes, I swear I could still see him and feel his body against mine. He was special to me. At one point in my life he was so familiar to me, I allowed him to share parts of me that I'd never shared with anyone else before him. Being that I was just seventeen when I met him I knew we couldn't be together and that wanting him was wrong, but I did. I wanted him. I wanted him so fucking bad. At that time, he was a mature thirty-year-old, married, father and up and coming businessman. Meanwhile, I was a mature and studious, senior in high school, on my way to college. I was very much sheltered and inexperienced.

I was a tall, curvy girl and fully developed for my age, my sturdy hour glass body standing five feet eight inches tall. My ass was firm and round and at seventeen my enlarged breasts were spilling out of my full-figured bras. My hips were wide, and I had a flat stomach which always made it difficult to find clothes that fit. Shopping for clothes was never fun. I rarely found clothes that fit my bottom half, but I always found a way to dress cute and classy for my body shape. My shape got a lot of men's attention from a young age. Young men, old men, creepy men and even the men who liked men. This was a challenge for me growing up. I was raised by my father after my mother died in the accident. My mother was beautiful and more voluptuous than me. It was hard for my dad, watching me as I grew into a modern version of my mother. I looked like her in the face and in the body. My dad hated that I was shaped like my mother because he knew the type of attention it drew from men and he always felt as though he had to be my bodyguard.

Growing up without my mom was really hard. Although my time with her was brief, the love we shared remains deep, guiding me through life's labyrinth. I remembered the joy she brought into our lives. Her infectious laughter, warm hugs, and tender words were like a blanket to my soul. Despite the hardships we faced, her unwavering love cast a golden hue over our lives, reminding us that even in the darkest moments, light could be found.

Every year on special occasions like Mother's Day, her birthday, my parents wedding anniversary and my birthday would be a sad time for me, when all the girls around me had the blessing of enjoying those times with their mothers. I tried not to let anyone know how I felt when those dates rolled around. I never wanted to seem ungrateful to the people who cared for me in her place, but a mother's love is irreplaceable. My mother had good taste in men because my father was really the best dad any girl could hope for. My dad kept my mother's memory alive by keeping a lot of photos of her around the house and always telling me things about her. No matter how busy he was, or how much he was traveling he made it to every recital, soccer game and anything else that it was important to me that he be there. On occasion Aunt Gigi would stand in for him, but he didn't make it a habit. He always wanted to be there for me.

CHAPTER TWO

After the accident my dad moved us to Atlanta, Georgia to be closer to my mother's family. More opportunities for black businessmen were emerging and my dad was going to need some help raising me because he didn't have any family, he grew up in foster care, and he had no clue about how to raise a daughter on his own. My aunt Gigi and Grandma Jean moved to Atlanta after grandpa Ethan died, a few years before the accident. After grandpa Ethan died grandma Jean retired from SEPTA and they moved to Atlanta, because that's where she grew up and wanted to spend her retirement. Also, because Grandma Jean was tired of the cold Pennsylvania winters. I remembered my mom being sad about them moving so far away. My mom was the youngest and she and Aunt Gigi were so close, and they are grandma's only children. I remembered being sad when they moved because I was also close to my aunt. But with my mom gone my dad was going to need some help raising me.

He bought a modern two-story home in Buckhead with a separate in law- suite from the main house, next to the pool. He bought this house for my Grandma Jean and Aunt Gigi to live with us. Grandma Jean still liked to stay at her own home, and she declined living with us, but my aunt Gigi lived in the in-law suite, so she was always there for us. My dad was just starting his investment company in Atlanta and he didn't know anything about raising a girl on his own, so he loved having Aunt Gigi around.

My aunt Gigi was very sentimental, and she was always sharing stories about my mom and my parents love story with me. My parents met in high school, they were ambitious and inseparable. They were their high school Homecoming King and Queen and prom King and Queen. After they graduated high school they planned to attend the same college because that's just how inseparable they were. Together they attended the Ivy League school, The University of Pennsylvania. My mother earned her bachelor's degree in Art History and my father earned his degree in Business Finance. They were married shortly after their college graduation. They like any other young couple struggled to pay the bills, but they were crazy in love and determined to be successful. They rented a small studio apartment in Center City Philadelphia, with no central heat or air, brown water running through the banging pipes and cracks in the hardwood floors. My mother took a job as a file clerk for the Philadelphia Art Museum and my father unhappily worked as a financial analyst for a small investment company in Philly named Goldstein & Levin Holdings. My dad was not happy working there, but it paid the bills.

They were married for two years before my mom got pregnant for the first time. My mom was pregnant with twin boys and they were both so excited about the twins and becoming parents. The day they found out it was twin boys they picked their names, Elton Jr. and Ethan. Elton after my dad and Ethan after my grandpa Ethan, my mom's dad. My mom had a rough pregnancy with preeclampsia and pain from her growing womb, and sadly she had a miscarriage in her second trimester. They were devastated but they didn't let that discourage them from trying again. They wanted children, they wanted a big family and they were ready to start their family. My dad wanted his children to have the family that he didn't. Then about a year after the miscarriage I came along, their wide eyed, chubby brown baby girl. Due to complications with my birth, my mother had to have a hysterectomy and it was determined that I would be an only child. Being their only child, I was spoiled with adoration from my parents.

During this time, when I still had both of my parents, my dad was working a lot trying to climb the corporate ladder and I spent most of my time with my mom. I enjoyed my childhood with her. My mom would spend hours crafting tales of transformers and princesses, exploring mystical realms woven from the threads of her boundless imagination. I was an adventurous kid, I was allowed to be myself, they both allowed me to explore my childhood curiosities. My parents were the best parents a girl could only hope for. My parents were the picture of black love, a testament to black strength and resilience, but everything changed the day of the accident. My father became a single father in an instant and he tried to make sure I never felt the absence of my mother. He included her in decisions to always remind me of what my mother would have said about any given situation. For instance, if I was wearing something too short he would remind me of what my mother would say about it. He was strict with me, always checking to know where I was and who I was with and he made sure I stayed out of trouble and kept my head on straight and in the books. He raised me to be a smart, mature and beautiful, woman, who up until I met him, was too focused on my education to be concerned with boys or a relationship. Boys didn't excite me like getting my education did. Not until I met him.

I was a straight A student at St. Bernadette's Catholic School. And, although by this time my father could afford to send me to any college or university I was accepted to, I wanted to earn an academic scholarship on my own. It was important to me. Up until this time, school was the most important thing to me, other than my family and friends. As I got older I wanted my independence and to experience life, like my friends. I wanted to get a job and make my own money. My dad was afraid that my education would suffer due to me working when he thought I should be studying, but I was determined to show him I could balance working a part-time job and still keep my grades up.

I had my first job at my aunt Gigi's hair salon when I was sixteen. She was like a mother to me, after my mom's passing my aunt stepped in like a fairy godmother, filling the void with her unwavering love and support. Her nurturing presence and compassionate nature made her feel like a second mother to me. She offered a listening ear, a comforting embrace, and a shoulder to cry on whenever I needed it. Through her constant presence and guidance, she helped me navigate the complexities of becoming a woman, reminding me that I was never alone. I am forever grateful for the impact she had on my life, forever cherishing her as a mother figure who will always hold a special place in my heart. I looked up to her for maternal support. As I got older she was there for me in ways my dad couldn't be. She was there to help me through those uncomfortable girl moments like my first period and the first time I got the embarrassing red dot on the back of my pants when sitting in public. I worked in my aunt's office after school and on weekends. The salon was always busy on the weekends. I loved being there with my aunt and I enjoyed hearing all the gossip. As I approached my senior year in high school I told my Aunt Gigi that I wanted to leave and get a real job. She was mad because I was her best and most trusted employee, but she let me go.

CHAPTER THREE

I started working a part-time job at Taylor's department store in the mall, the summer before senior year of high school. I wanted the job at Taylor's because it was a trendy store, a lot of my friends worked at the mall and all mall employees received a twenty percent discount on everything and even though I wore a uniform to school I liked to look fly when I was hanging out.

I worked because I wanted to do things for myself and it was a way for me to get out of the house and socialize while earning some cash. I craved my independence. I enjoyed working and earning my own money and not having to always ask my dad for things all the time. No teenage girl wants to have to ask her dad or anyone else to buy her feminine products. I worked at the perfume counter at Taylor's, a few days a week after school and on weekends making ten dollars an hour. Being able to work and keep my four point zero grade point average was still important to me, so there were many nights when I was up late studying after I got home from work.

I'd had the same two besties since the ninth grade, and I felt like I didn't hang out with them anymore as it got closer to graduation. Joanna was calm and composed, she was raised by a single mother and had to help take care of her family. She was the go-to person whenever there was a need for a heartfelt conversation or a new idea. Angie was my closer and more outgoing friend, who was always chasing boys. Angie could be wild, she brought zest and excitement to the group and she liked to test boundaries. I was kind of in the middle of them. I for the most part was reserved and calm, but I was outspoken, and I had my bold side too. I was the think it through, level headed friend. Together, we formed a tight-knit circle, supporting and uplifting each other throughout our high school journey. Our differences complemented one another, creating a diverse and well-rounded group of dynamic young women. Whether it was celebrating successes, navigating challenges, or simply enjoying each other's company, our friendship was a cherished and integral part my high school experience. Senior year was the year that we didn't have any classes together. I drove my dad's old Toyota Camry. So, on the days when I was running late for work it was usually because I was hanging out after school in the senior parking lot running my mouth and catching up with the girls. I really hated to be late so if I didn't have enough time to change my clothes into my work uniform I would just wear my school uniform to work.

The day I met him was one of those days where I was chatting with my girls after school and then had to rush off to work, praying I didn't get a speeding ticket. I always clocked in with minutes to spare and the customers never complained that I was not in the store uniform, if anything it got me more sales. The women would see me in my school uniform and spark up a conversation around school and their children and the men liked to see a Catholic school girl in a short skirt. I wore my hair long with just the ends of my hair in big curls pulled back with a black plastic headband. My white round collared short sleeve shirt was embroidered with **SBCS** for St. Bernadette's Catholic School on the side of each sleeve, paired with my burgundy plaid skirt romper and block loafers that lifted me up about two inches. I was already five foot eight and pretty sure I was the tallest I would ever be. I'd been the exact same height for three years. Although, my breasts kept getting bigger. I always wanted big breasts until I got them. Sometimes I wouldn't realize my breasts were getting bigger until they began to create huge gaps in between the buttons of my school uniform blouse. I'd exposed myself several times and been mortified each time.

The first time I had an embarrassing breast exposing moment was at the beginning of my ninth-grade year. I for the most part was a quiet girl and had a closer relationship with my journal than people. I was walking into class when I saw Anthony, a boy I'd had a crush on since the first day of high school. We approached the science room door at the same time, and he spoke to me, uttering the words, "Hi, you can go", and I smiled at him, with my head down, walking fast, past him into the classroom to my seat, too shy to give a response. That was the first time he talked to me. Once I sat at my table I felt dazed, considering all of the responses I should have given to Anthony. I had to quickly overcome my shyness if I was going to get his attention. I wanted him to ask me for my phone number because I wanted to get to know him. The next day I saw him in the hallway headed into class, I sped up walking briskly through the narrow and crowded hallway, so it appeared just like the first time we approached the classroom door at the same time, but this time he didn't speak, he just walked ahead of me into the crowded classroom. I walked into the full chemistry class and that's when it happened. I didn't know why, but everyone in the class was staring at me and laughing. There were a lot of students in the room. I followed their eyes and saw they were all laughing at my exposed breasts. I had popped the button on my shirt and revealed my granny bra. Apparently my blouse popped open while I was briskly walking to class and I didn't realize it until everyone was laughing. I was so embarrassed. I was wearing an old Playtex bra with no under wire that my grandma Jean gave me as a hand me down. It was a beige bra with circus clowns and colorful triangle and circle shapes on it. The bra was too small, and my breasts were spilling over in it. I snatched my shirt closed with my hands and held it together like the jaws of life and sat on the high stool along the lab table in the back of the classroom. I was so embarrassed I was in tears. A girl in the back of the class who also had the blessing and the curse of having big full breasts handed me her burgundy school uniform sweater. I threw that ugly sweater on gratefully still fighting back the tears as the teacher walked in and gained control of the rowdy classroom. That's how I met Angie and we became friends. From then on I made sure to wear a cute bra, just in case my shirt opened unexpectedly again.

CHAPTER FOUR

It was usually just me and another employee, my co-worker Sheila to work the perfume counter on week-nights. Sheila was an older woman, a single mom with two kids who was always on her cell phone. She was short and round always complaining about her weight, but always in the food court. I didn't like her because she would disappear after she clocked in and make me do all the work.

 It was a Friday evening after school and the store was full of holiday shoppers. I always was the one to organize the mess of perfume sample cards and tester bottles thrown all over the rectangle shaped glass counter, left over from the day shift.

The repetitive holiday music was in an obnoxious rotation, with Mariah Carey's All I Want for Christmas leading the medley. I was wearing my school uniform, organizing the sample bottles of Chanel, that's when I saw him approaching the perfume counter. He caught my attention as I was looking up, organizing the display shelf behind the sales counter and I couldn't take my eyes off of him. The closer he came towards me the hotter my body became. He was gorgeous, like a model off of the cover of GQ magazine. He moved with confidence and he had a sexy walk that commanded your attention. His dark hair was cut low, a salt and pepper goatee, his thick neck nestled under his navy-blue striped tie. His smooth chocolate pecan brown skin pressed against his tailored dark gray suit looks picturesque. He wore multicolored socks that played peek-a-boo with each step down the hard floors, adding an element of fun to the professional playfulness about him. He adjusted his glasses on his nose as he approached the neat perfume counter. "Hi", he said so charismatically with his big hands on the glass counter. I on the other hand couldn't think of the words to say and I stood there with a silent girlish grin. It was like meeting Anthony in the ninth grade all over again, I thought. I paused too long and just blurted out "Welcome to Taylor's where we Tailor your experience." I said biting and wetting my lips.

"I don't mean to be rude so please don't take this the wrong way", he said clearing his throat. I was curious to know what he was going to say. I still didn't say a word I just gave him the look that he could tell me. "Your blouse is open", he said. I looked down and saw indeed my third button had come undone and my cleavage was exposed in my white lace Victoria's Secret bra. I immediately turned my back to him to button my shirt closing the gap in my blouse. I was so embarrassed. That had not happened in a long time. Why now in front of this man, I thought? He too looked embarrassed. "I'm sorry I wasn't being a pervert", he said apologetically. "I just saw you and I noticed your", he clears his throat, "you know" he said taking his finger and pointing at my now covered breasts." I wasn't looking. I mean", he paused "I was", he corrected.

"I'm so embarrassed," I said covering my face and my smile with the palms of my hands. "Don't cover up your smile you have nothing to be ashamed of. Your body is beautiful", he said taking my hand into his.

For a moment I blushed, my brown skin became flushed and we remained silent just exchanging energy through the touch of our hands until I abruptly snatched my hand away from him. I looked beyond his sculpted shoulders and saw a familiar man approaching us, with the clack of his expensive shoes slowing down against the tiled floor.

I recognized the other man as he approached the counter. "There's my baby girl", he said embracing me as I stepped in front of the perfume counter. I felt the other man's eyes explore my body as my thick lower half was revealed from around the counter.

"Hi daddy!", I said with a smile. "What are you doing in the mall? You never come to the mall", I said nervously trying not to make eye contact with the man in the gray suit.

My dad laughed placing his hand on the other man's shoulder. "Well, for one thing I wanted to pick up a Christmas gift for your aunt Gigi and I wanted my new business partner to meet you." My dad turned to him to introduce us. "Londyn, meet Victor Crawford, our newest senior investment banker. Victor meet my one and only baby girl Londyn Banks", he said smiling at me proudly.

"Londyn Banks that's a beautiful name", Victor said, taking my hand in his and kissing the back of my hand like a gentleman. I felt a sensation like an electrical current wave through my body as I tried to keep my dad from recognizing my temperature rising for that man. My dad didn't sense a thing and he excitedly continued to tell me how he recently hired Victor after head hunting him from a competitor and all the big things they planned to do together. Then he told me to pick out some perfume that my Aunt Gigi would like and to also select something for Victor's wife as a Christmas gift. I abruptly stopped and looked up at Victor, quickly acknowledging and adjusting my reaction so my dad didn't notice. I hadn't paid attention to the ring on his finger. I smiled, rolled my eyes and told my dad "I have just the scent for you both and I grabbed a bottle of Beautiful by Estee Lauder and told them, "Tell them how *Beautiful* they smell. Older women love this fragrance", I added. I turned to get the other bottle from the storage cabinet, and I told them their total. My dad tells Victor he's paying for it all and blurted, "Merry Christmas."

I handed him his wife's gift in the yellow paper bag and told him "I hope your wife enjoys it. I know my aunt Gigi will." My dad's phone rang, and he answered it. It had something to do with business, while on the phone my dad gave me a hug and kissed me on the cheek, "We have to go. I'll see you later baby girl. You be safe" he said to me and he and Victor left. I wanted Victor to look back at me, but he didn't, and I watched him walk away, disappearing beyond the Men's department. Once I stood alone at the counter I felt my panties were moist. My life with Victor flashed before my eyes and I thought of nothing else for the rest of the night. I was grateful when the cash register didn't come up short because for the rest of my shift I couldn't concentrate on anything but the lingering memory and the feeling of him.

I went home and wrote about him in my journal that night. From that night on I began to tuck my journal in my pillow case.

CHAPTER FIVE

I had feelings for Victor that I had never felt with anyone before. With Victor working so closely with my dad I knew I would see him again and that thought excited me. For the next few days I couldn't get him out of my mind. I was sitting at the dinner table with dad and Aunt Gigi when his cell phone resting on the table began to ring.

He put down his wine glass to answer his phone with a big smile on his face. "Victor tell me you have great news." He said loudly, as he finished chewing his food and paused to listen. After a few uncertain nods my dad's facial expressions let us know this was a good call. "Wonderful! I'll get the papers drafted in the morning!", my dad replied

"Dad what has you so happy?", I questioned inquisitively.

"That was Victor, you met him at the store the other day. He just acquired another multi-million-dollar account", he told us wearing a big grin. "Victor is just what we needed to enter the commercial real estate investing space. Our profit margins are going to be higher than ever!", my dad exclaimed.

I sat across from my dad trying to hold back excitement at the sound of Victor's name. "That's great dad!"

"Victor is just what I needed to advance the company. We must celebrate when I see him tomorrow," he explained.

"Tomorrow is Saturday, dad. You're going to the office?" I questioned.

"No, baby girl, the Christmas party is tomorrow evening, and everyone will be there", he explained.

My stomach felt like the drop of a roller coaster as I nervously asked my dad if I could go to the party.

He was surprised that I even wanted to go since I've never had an interest in going to any company events before. He welcomed the idea of me going to the party. I caught my aunt Gigi looking at me from the corner of her eyes trying to figure out what I was up to.

It was at the company Christmas party the next day that I saw him again. I arrived attached to my dad's arm wearing a white halter cocktail dress that squeezed my ample breasts in a way that made sure you noticed them. I spotted Victor, from across the room as soon as we arrived. I stayed close to my dad because I wanted Victor to see me. It didn't take long. Just like I thought, Victor saw my dad and began to approach us, only he wasn't alone. An attractive woman was walking very close to him, coming towards us.

"Elton I see you made it to the festivities," Victor said to my dad. Then he turned to the woman "Honey, this is Elton Banks the CEO and Chairman of the Board of E.J. Banks Capital Inc and this is his lovely daughter Londyn", he then put his arm around his wife "and this is my lovely wife Lisa", he continued.

"It's a pleasure to meet you and your little girl", she said smiling at us.

I was standing there admiring her and pulling her apart in every comparison. My hair is long, her hair is short, she's round and short, I'm tall and thick. Little girl, I repeated to myself raging on the inside. This little girl will steal your man, I said silently cocky. I wanted to see in her what he saw in her. She was pretty I'll give him that, but I definitely looked better than her. Her hair was in small Sister locks, and she wore a flowing dress to hide her pudgy stomach. She was okay, but I felt he could do better, and I was better.

My dad continued on rambling and I zoned back into the conversation. "My daughter Londyn is a senior at St. Bernadette's and she will be leaving us and going off to college soon." I smiled as my dad bragged about me. "I didn't have a boy so one day my baby girl is going to take over the business." I smiled and looked away because I had no desire to take do what my dad does.

Victor looked at me in awe. I looked at Victor's wife and told her she smells beautiful. His wife looked at me with an uncertain look. Victor cleared his throat and excuses them, "Nice to meet you" she said as they walked away into the crowd and onto the dance floor as they slow danced to smooth jazz holiday music. My eyes followed them all night. I watched how he looked at her while they danced. I noted how he held her and how his body moved with hers. He was a great dancer. He must have felt my eyes on them because all night he kept staring back at me. After I'd had enough of watching them together I went for a walk outside. I needed some fresh air, I felt like I was suffocating in there. I was standing outside lost in my own thoughts and the swirl of emotions around my heart. He saw me standing alone along the walkway and he stood beside me.

"What are you doing out here?", Victor asked.

"I just needed some air", I admitted. He put his arm around me and pulled me to his side. He whispered to me "Girl if you were legal I might be in trouble". My heart jolted and I had to remind myself to breathe. I whispered back to him, "If you weren't married you might be in trouble." He looked down at me, releasing his embrace and walked back inside before someone came looking for us. I went home that night and wrote another entry about Victor in my journal.

CHAPTER SIX

Christmas day marked exactly three months until my eighteenth birthday. Christmas was me and my mom's favorite holiday. I loved that time of the year with all the lights and festivities. I spent Christmas morning opening gifts and eating with my dad, Aunt Gigi and Grandma Jean. On days like this I really missed my mom. The Christmas before she died I made a glass Christmas ornament as part of my art class project to give to her as a Christmas gift. It was a circular clear glass ornament that I painted in a white iridescent glitter glue with two white turtle doves and white sparkling glitter inside and when you shook it up it created snow around the birds. After we finished opening all the gifts I took the ornament off of the tree and sat outside by the pool staring at the ornament with tears in my eyes as I remembered Christmas with my mom.

My mom's name was Jeanette Banks, she was beautiful, super smart and funny. My mom loved being a mother, all she ever wanted was a family of her own. Because I was an only child I got all my mom's attention. She was like my best friend. She was the first person I wanted to show when I learned something, or I accomplished something new. I remembered when I gave her the Christmas ornament. I remember the day we were to bring them home I was scared I was going to break it if I rode home on the bus with it. I was in the second grade and I asked my teacher if I could go to the front office to use the phone to call my mom. She told me we could only go to the office to use the phone was if it was an emergency. So, I lied and said it was an emergency. My teacher gave me the hall pass and I walked to the office. I was going to tell my mom the truth that it wasn't an emergency, but I needed a ride home because I was afraid I would break my ornament on the bus. When I got to the office and told Ms. Andress at the front desk that I needed to use the phone she reminded me the phone was only for students with emergencies. I again lied and said it was an emergency. Now, Ms. Andress was paying attention to my every word and move, and I knew I had to continue the lie when my mom answered the phone. I had to think quick on my feet for a seven year old and I thought back to a time my mom called out of work because she forgot to request off the day of my field trip to the zoo. I heard her tell her manager she was sick, and she had cramps. So, that's what my young mind came up with and I told my mom I had cramps. She sounded shocked and asked me what hurt, and I told her my head hurt. Ms. Andress looked at me and asked me if I knew what cramps were and I answered her "Yes", with a snarky attitude and I rubbed my head. Not long afterwards my mom arrived at the school and found me in the front office with a very confused and concerned Ms. Andress. My mom looked just as confused as Ms. Andress and asked me if I noticed anything in my panties. I was so embarrassed and confused I really didn't understand why she was asking me that. My mom took me to the class to get my bookbag, my coat and the Christmas ornament. As soon as we got in the car my mom began grilling me about having cramps. I couldn't keep up the lie and before we got out of the school zone I confessed to lying, but I didn't even tell her about the ornament I just told her I really wanted to come home and I apologized for lying. My mom seemed relieved and she laughed. I was glad she didn't whoop my ass for making her leave work because I lied. I wanted her to be completely shocked when she saw the ornament I made for her. Christmas morning after I opened all my gifts I ran to my room and got the ornament from under my bed where I was hiding it and handed it to my mom. Then I confessed the real reason I had cramps at school. Oh, she laughed and laughed. She promised to decorate the tree with the ornament every year. That was the only year she saw the tree decorated with the ornament. I stared at the ornament in my hands thinking back to a time where blood flowed through my mother's veins as she held that ornament in her hands. Londyn, I thought to myself as I wiped the tears from my eyes, get a grip this is supposed to be a happy day. I pushed out that bittersweet memory. I looked down at my hammer toes and thought back to the time when I told her I wanted to take ballet lessons. She was excited at the idea of me in ballet school and enrolled me. Even though I was bigger than all the girls in the class she was always so encouraging. She never let me get discouraged because of my size. My mom was the loudest one in the room, cheering me on at all of my recitals. When I would be on stage I would look off in the distance so I wouldn't get distracted by my mom who was mirroring the choreography from the front row. Sometimes my dad was too busy, but my mom was always there. My mom was the kind of mom who worked all day, came home to cook dinner and helped me with my homework and was there for every school activity or performance. On the weekends I would be awakened by the sounds of Toni Braxton's CD skipping and the smell of bacon cooking. She was like super woman to me and my parents maintained a loving relationship. I never understood how she did it all. She always had a way to make you laugh but get her point across. Don't get me wrong there were the times that I was being a kid and my mom took my dad's belt off and whooped my ass. The most vivid memories I had of her were from the day of the accident. To me that morning started off just like any other morning. Mom cooked breakfast for me, and I sat and ate at the table while she drank her coffee trying to get herself and my dad dressed and out of the apartment. My mother was running late to drop me off to school due to suffering from another intense migraine. All that morning she kept holding her head in pain and I remember she kept asking me to repeat things. We were almost to my school when my mother suddenly slumped over and lost control of the steering wheel, the car flipped off the highway going about sixty miles per hour, northbound on The Boulevard. I was seated in the back seat of the black Nissan Maxima, with my seat belt on. I was lucky to be alive and I was banged up pretty bad. I broke my left leg, fractured my ribs from the impact of the seatbelt and I had to have stitches over my right eyebrow. My mother experienced the worst impact from the accident. She was ejected from the car, landing on the concrete and was rushed to Einstein hospital in critical condition. There she had a CAT scan that revealed that she had a massive brain tumor. She was diagnosed with Glioblastoma, an aggressive form of brain cancer. This was the cause for her migraines and memory loss, which caused her to black out moments before the accident. The doctors gave her just a few short days to live. She never left the hospital. My mother died November 7, 1989. I was just eight years old. As I got older the holidays never got easier.

Later on, Christmas day I was standing in the kitchen, drying the breakfast dishes with my grandma and Aunt Gigi when my dad walked in and told us some people from the office may stop by later on that day. My heart fluttered and I perked up. I tried not to show my excitement, but I was excited and anxious, and I needed to get upstairs I hadn't even taken a shower. I dried my hands on the festive dish towel, thinking I was about to leave when my grandma called me out. "Genevieve where does this girl think she's going?", my grandma asked my aunt who was standing there cutting her eyes at me.

 "Grandma I represent daddy I can't have his colleagues seeing me like this. I look a mess." I kissed my grandma on the cheek and ran upstairs as only I could get away with that, leaving them to finish putting away the dishes. The truth was, I was hoping one of the colleagues would be Victor. I changed into something flattering and mature hoping to get Victor's attention. I put on a long hunter green spaghetti strapped dress. Nothing fancy, but I wanted to get his attention, but of all the people from the office who came Victor was not one of them. I spent the rest of the day swimming in my own thoughts. Thoughts about being with him, why didn't he come and what his reaction would have been had he seen me in my dress.

I spent the next few days of Christmas break submitting my college admissions applications and waiting for their responses. I had narrowed it down to Florida A&M University, Columbia University and The University of Pennsylvania. I purposefully chose all out of state colleges. I felt that was my only way to release my dad's overprotective grip on me. I hadn't seen Victor since the Christmas party.

 For the next few weeks Victor and my dad were often traveling together, and I hadn't seen him, but I thought about Victor every day. I was even considering changing to an in-state college just to be closer to him.

Love was in the air as Valentine's Day rolled around. All I could do was think about Victor. The guys at my high school knew they didn't have a chance with me, I had been turning them down for four years. I was surprised as I sat in Ms. Parker's AP Lit class when I received an unexpected arrival. A man in an orange uniform shirt walked in the class and handed me a dozen red roses. Everyone in the class was staring at me including Ms. Parker. The delivery man left the chatty classroom and my teacher turned her eyes to me. "Now that Ms. Banks is finished disturbing my lesson let's continue with the discussion about Sethe and slavery's destruction of her identity," she commanded control of her class. I noticed a card in the middle of the bouquet and I inconspicuously opened the tiny card that read. *Happy Valentine's Day Londyn!* It wasn't signed by anyone the senders section on the card was left blank. I wondered who sent me the flowers. I thought about Victor, but he was in Dubai with my dad. That afternoon I met up with my friends, Joanna and Angie in the senior parking lot. They heard about my flower delivery before I could even tell them. Angie's boyfriend only gave her a card and Joanna didn't have a boyfriend or a secret admirer, so they were both envious of my flowers. That day after school I left my friends in enough time to clock in on time. About an hour into my shift I saw the same delivery man in the orange shirt walking through the department store. I wondered who he was there to deliver to this time. This time I noticed he had a bigger bouquet that looked like two dozen roses. The delivery man walked closer to my counter and stopped when he saw me. "It's you again" he laughed handing me the large bouquet of red roses. "Thank you" I replied. I was embarrassed at the attention it drew to me. I began looking through the flowers for the card. I found the card in the large bouquet. This time written on the card was *I can't get you off my mind* and nothing else. Again, the from section was left blank. All the women were staring at me as I placed the large bouquet on the glass counter.

"Londyn who are they from?" Sheila asked me.

"I don't know", I replied. "The same deliveryman delivered flowers to me at school earlier today, but the card doesn't say who they are from", I said admiring the fragrant petals. "Hmph," she scoffed. "Somebody must have a secret admirer", she said pulling one of the flowers out of the bouquet and brought it to her nose. "My no-good baby daddy never gave me shit and I had his babies. What did you do to get those?", she looked at me with one eyebrow up. I picked up the flowers from the glass counter and replied, "Nothing at all" and I carried the flowers over to the display case with the new Runwayvixxen fragrance Sweetlicious and fanned out the flowers to add some attention to the display. I made more in commission that day than ever before.

I went home that night carrying in three dozen roses up to my room one at a time. My aunt Gigi saw me bring in the last bouquet and questioned who sent me the flowers. I told her I didn't know, and she too looked at me in surprise and reminded me that I better not let my dad see them. That night as I laid amongst the rose petals I wrote in my journal, wondering if the roses were a gift from Victor.

CHAPTER SEVEN

It was coming up on my eighteenth birthday on March twenty fifth and I still didn't know what I wanted to do for my birthday. Everyone kept asking me what I wanted but I didn't know how to respond. The only thing I really wanted was a new car. I was still driving the 1994 Honda Civic that I got for my sixteenth birthday. I wanted to ask for a newer car, but I knew my dad wasn't going to buy me a new car. Eventually they all stopped asking me about what I wanted for my birthday. The day of my birthday my dad instructed me to come right home after school. Being that my birthday was on a Friday I swung by Taylor's department store and picked up my paycheck first. What I didn't know was my dad, Aunt Gigi, Grandma Jean and my besties Angie and Joanna were waiting for me at my house to shout, "Surprise! ", at me. I saw their cars, even some cars I didn't recognize in the horseshoe driveway when I pulled up to my house, so I was pretty sure they were all there for my birthday, I just played along. Like expected I walked in my front door and it was expectedly silent. I walked past my mother's urn and photo hanging by the front entrance, through the downstairs hallway with my chunky heels striking the floors. I walked into the kitchen and almost swallowed my gum. I anticipated the surprise but not him to be there. I walked into my kitchen where my dad was blowing through a party streamer and my Aunt Gigi, my grandma Jean, my besties and the gorgeous Victor Crawford shouted happy birthday to me! My dad walked over to me, pulled the metallic party streamer from his mouth and kissed me on the cheek. "I can't believe my baby girl is all grown up!" he said holding me by my shoulders. "It's like just yesterday you were an infant laying on your mother's chest. Time stands still for no man." My dad was beginning to get emotional and I saw him fighting back tears in his eyes but maintained his sharp demeanor. My aunt Gigi who was teary eyed and looking like my mom took my hand, pulled me away from my dad and hugged me. "My sister would have been so proud of you Londyn", she said. "You want to know why my sister wanted to call you Londyn?", she paused. "Because when we were little girls, we lived in a one bed room, one-bathroom apartment in Philly and we had this tree outside of our apartment building and we would climb up that tree every chance we could. I would climb to the top of the small sap tree that was like our pretend club house and your mom would be up there with me pretending we were famous models and we would be lost in our own little world for hours. We would pretend that we had English accents and our tree was London bridge and London bridge is what took us from poverty to our make-believe luxurious life. She always wanted to travel to London in person, but she never made it there", tears began to glide down Aunt

Gigi's rouge cheeks. I grabbed a paper towel from
the kitchen island and handed it to my aunt. As I was
consoling my emotional aunt, I saw my two friends
standing around laughing at me. I was the last one of
my friends to turn eighteen and this was by far the
worst party. For Joanna's eighteenth birthday her
mom threw her a party at the Stanford hotel, in
downtown Atlanta and after the party we stayed at
the hotel overnight. Just me and Angie stayed
overnight. Joanna's mom and step-dad stayed in a
room on the floor above us. We could order all the
room service and rent all the movies we wanted. We
had a great time and I knew Angie would try to one
up Joanna. For Angie's birthday last month her
parents rented a yacht on Lake Lanier and invited
half the senior class. Angie's boyfriend Ryan brought
a bottle of tequila to the party and everybody got
wasted. I never told my dad what I wanted to do for
my birthday. After while I could tell he had
something planned because he kept reminding me
not to plan anything on my birthday and he was
being super secretive, taking calls in the other room
and hanging up the phone when he heard me. That
was very unlike my dad to behave like that around
me. My dad and I had very open communication.
Sometimes, too open, but that's how I knew
something was going on. He seemed excited about
whatever he was planning for my eighteenth birthday.
It was like he had been planning for the day my
whole life. And it wasn't until recently that I decided
what I wanted for my birthday. What I wanted was

standing at the end of the kitchen island talking to my dad but looking at me out of the corner of his dark brown eyes. Once he saw that he had my attention he walked over to me. I watched how he walked over to me leaning toward me to embrace me. My aunt Gigi stood up to get his attention, she was much older than Victor, but she was youthful and beautiful. If he recognized her sudden flirtatious behavior he didn't react to it because his eyes were glued to my mature body.

"Happy Birthday!" he smiled and hugged me with one arm over my shoulder. "Were you surprised?" he asked me with one thick eyebrow up, his eyes glaring at me.

"Are you asking if I was surprised about my party or are you asking if I'm surprised that you are at my surprise party celebrating my birthday with me?" He smiled at me and I felt electricity travel through my veins. He handed me a small card with my name written on the front of the purple envelope. I stared at the card wondering what was inside. What would he have given an eighteen-year-old girl for her birthday, I questioned? I didn't know what he was giving to me, but I knew what I wanted him to take. I got ready to open the small envelope when he pushed my hand down and he told me to open it later. I wanted to open it right then because I was anxious to know what awaited me inside, but suddenly the kitchen light was turned off and my dad walked out with a round three tier cake with pink and purple icing spelling Happy Birthday Londyn, with burning candle wax dripping on the cake. I stood there embarrassed, leaning on the counter as everyone gathered around and stared at me as they all sang an off-key version of the happy birthday song. I covered my face in embarrassment. Once they were done I yelled "OK, enough it's time to cut the cake!" I cut my cake into small slices and enjoyed my sweet indulgence. I wanted to be his sweet indulgence and not the cake, but I handed him a paper plate with a moist slice of cake with colorful icing, some of which I got on my thumb and I made sure that he was watching me lick the icing from my finger. He blushed, trying not to make eye contact. I had not eaten much since I was dieting to fit into my prom dress in just a few weeks, but I ate a slice and I made sure he saw me lick the fork clean. I didn't have a prom date and neither did Joanna, so we decided we'd just go together. I still wanted to look amazing in my dress for the pictures.

After cake, my dad was ready to give me my birthday gifts. I wasn't expecting much. I had most things that I wanted. My dad tapped his fork against his glass and began to give a speech, further embarrassing me. "Londyn I am so proud of the young woman you've become. You've not only had to learn how to be a woman without a mother's guidance, you are a beautiful black woman, you are a straight A student, you've been accepted to every college you've applied to," he paused.

"Well not yet", I injected anxiously. I was still waiting to hear from one school.

"Your mother would have been so proud of you", he took a deep breath looking over at my Aunt Gigi. "Baby girl, I'm so proud of you, I been waiting a long time for this day that I hoped would take an eternity to come but I have something's for you." My dad reached in the drawer and handed me two letters one opened and one sealed letter. "What is this?" I questioned until I saw the opened letter was from the University of Pennsylvania. It was my final admissions letter and the one I was waiting for. I was jumping up and down. My besties were not as excited for me. They were both going to in-state colleges. They were both accepted to Spelman. I knew that if I stayed too close to my dad he would never let me grow up and he would treat me like his little girl forever. I looked up at my dad realizing he opened the letter and he knew the status of my admission. But then I remembered there were two letters. I hurried to open the first one. I opened the unsealed envelope first reading just the first sentence before I was screaming and again jumping up and down.

Ms. Londyn Banks,

Congratulations! It is with great pleasure that I inform you that you have been accepted for admission to The University of Pennsylvania fall semester with a full academic scholarship upon maintaining a 3.75 GPA or higher.

I was ecstatic! The University of Pennsylvania was my top choice. My parents graduated from the University of Pennsylvania and it meant a lot to me to go to my parent's alma mater and to be a legacy student. The room flooded with the harmonies of congratulations and hugs. I was so excited I was smiling from ear to ear. In the midst of the excitement I remembered there were two envelopes. I looked down at the light granite counter top at the unopened envelope. I took the dated envelope in my hands. The room got quiet. I read every word and number on the outside of the yellowish envelope, noticing the familiar handwriting. I gently tore the envelope open and pulled out the papers. The first paper was a hand-written letter from my mother. I read the letter silently, with tears streaming down my bronzed cheeks as those around me watched me silently read.

My Beautiful Londyn,

I love you! I love you! I love you! If you are reading this my body is not there with you, but my spirit lives inside you.

When I was told I only had a short time to live I wrote this letter to you. Please forgive me for leaving you so soon. My mind is strong, but my body has let me down. I wanted nothing more than to be your mother and to love you. I pray that you will have an amazing and fulfilling life. I want you to know that I love you more than all the grains of sand along the Atlantic Coast. I know you are going to grow up to

be beautiful with a smart mouth and a sharp mind. I
know this because you're my daughter. I want to be
there with you. I wanted to be the one to show you
how to do your makeup, prepare you for
womanhood, get you ready for prom, graduation,
your wedding and all the moments in between and
beyond. I wanted to be the one to hold you when
you're sad or scared. I have so much I want to say to
you. You come from a long line of strong women.
Be fearless as you embark on your life. You have an
inner strength that runs deep. Your veins are the
roots of your ancestors. Always remember your most
powerful tool is your mind however you choose to
use it makes it a weapon. I was the first woman in
our entire family to graduate from college and I want
you to be my legacy. It is my dying wish that you
grow up to understand the importance of educating
yourself and that you graduate from college, any
college you choose. I know you will grow up to be an
intelligent and beautiful black woman, part of my
legacy is going to be building your financial future.

I love my husband Elton Banks with my heart and
soul, I leave you both as the beneficiaries of my life
insurance policy. To my husband I leave the value of
my life insurance policy less one hundred thousand
dollars, to which shall be put in a trust to pay
Londyn's college expenses. The trust shall be
disbursed to you upon your college entrance with
one hundred percent of the remaining balance paid
to you upon college graduation. I pray that what you
will have in my absence will bring you comfort. I

promise to be present with you even when you think I'm not. You are the best part of me, and I loved every moment of being your mom.

I love you forever and ever always,

Mom

My heart skipped a beat when I saw the date the letter was written. She wrote the letter on the same day she died. Tears were streaming from my eyes, creating wet black race tracks down my bronzed cheeks. I was still silently reading every letter on the page as I heard my dad explaining to everyone that I was reading the letter my mother wrote to me on her deathbed. I laid the handwritten notarized letter on the counter and began to silently read over the next page. It was a copy of the beneficiary application for Radeco Insurance Company, in my mother's handwriting. Like the letter, the handwriting was shaky, which was unlike the handwriting I'd seen from my mother on the back of photos, inside greeting cards and other letters and notes she left behind. On the date the trust was started it was valued for one hundred thousand dollars. Oh my God that's a lot of money, I make less than five hundred a month working at Taylor's department store, I thought to myself. I turned the page, placing the second page on the counter top. I looked over the paper, initially unsure of what I was looking at. Then I saw the page header and I saw it was a projection statement from Radeco Insurance Company. The projection statement was future dated for my eighteenth birthday to have an estimated value of two hundred thousand dollars. My dad standing there with tears flooding his eyes slides me an unfolded, recent insurance statement on the counter in front of me. I slowly picked the paper up and shouted, "Oh Shit!" the balance in the policy as of the market closing on my eighteenth birthday had grown to a value of two hundred and fifty thousand dollars. My emotions were tangled in my stomach like a ball of yarn. My dad would always tell the story of how he started his company with the money he inherited from his wife's death. He never said anything about money left over for me. He never mentioned any of this. I would have given up every penny to have my mother there instead. In that moment I really missed my mom and I looked over to my Aunt Gigi who was balling her eyes out as she relived her last moments with her baby sister. I hugged my Aunt Gigi, pressing my wet cheek to hers, I was so emotional.

My friends finally came over towards me looking shocked.

"Ok, bitch you win!" Angie whispered.

"Are you ok?" Joanna asked emotionally supportive. "That was pretty heavy," she added.

"Yeah that was a lot", Angie inserted.

"I'm cool", I lied looking at my dad approaching me. My dad walked over to me to embrace me with a congratulations hug and handed me a jewelry box.

"Dad was this really the last thing mom did before she died?" I asked anchored to his response.

"Yes, it was", my dad replied. "Now you understand why I always pushed you so hard about getting your education. That's all your mother wanted for you. She would not let go until she knew this plan was in place for you. Then she made out with me one last time, and then," he said somberly, "until her oxygen levels got too low. They removed my lips from hers and replaced them with an oxygen mask. Moments later she was gone" he thought back to those last moments with his wife.

I was in no way prepared for all this and I didn't know how much more I could handle. I looked at the small, worn burgundy jewelry box in my hands. I'd never seen it before. My dad informed me the box was my mother's and it originally belonged to my maternal grandma. I opened the box and looked inside, finding two keys. One key on a key ring and one key on a silver necklace. I looked up at my dad unsure of what I was looking at both keys appeared to be car keys. My dad took a deep breath and sighed. "The silver necklace was the first gift I gave your mother for Mother's Day. The key on the necklace belonged to your mother. It's the key to the car she was driving when the accident happened. I looked down at the key in the palm of my hand and my dad took it if from my hands and gently placed the silver necklace around my neck with the key laying against my heart. "Before your mother died she told me she was grateful for the accident because it allowed her to enjoy her last moments on earth with us. Without the car accident revealing the brain tumor she may have just suddenly died and we wouldn't have had the opportunity to have closure. Your mother was at peace when she died because she knew you were going to be okay." I held the key in my hand as my dad secured the clasp around my neck. I never knew my dad had this.

"I hope you find comfort in knowing your mother is always with you as you begin your own journey through life", he said admiring the key around my neck. I looked over and Aunt Gigi is again balling her eyes out. I wiped the tears from my moist lashes, and I held up the other key questioning its significance. My dad then tells me "Oh that key is for your new mustang outside."

"You mean the other car in the drive-way that I saw when I pulled up is mine?" I exclaimed, looking at my friends. I guess my birthday wasn't so bad after all. I wiped my eyes and gathered all my letters including my purple card from Victor and I ran outside to admire my new car. It was brand new with less than twenty miles on it. It was a two door, mustang convertible with a burgundy body and a black drop top. I sat in the car and placed the purple card, my mother's letters and the acceptance letter in the passenger seat. My friends jumped in the back seat acting as if we were about to go on a road trip. I pulled out of the driveway and drove around the subdivision a few times, showing off my new car to the neighborhood.

I drove around the neighborhood passing the house a few times and then took a quick ride to Phipps Plaza to show off my new ride before I pulled back in the driveway.

It was getting late and my grandma Jean was getting ready to leave when we pulled up to the house from our joy ride.

"You young ladies have a blessed night and be safe getting home", my grandma told them while getting in her navy-blue Cadillac. I knew that meant it was time for my friends to go home. I turned the car, leaving the key in the ignition and walked my friends to their cars, promising to hit them up if I decided to do something later that night. We took one selfie together before they each pulled off in their cars. Once the driveway was cleared from their cars Victor walked up to me. "So, were you surprised?", he asked me again, this time alone. "Yes, and yes" I answered him flirtatiously. "I wasn't expecting any of this. This was the biggest surprise I could ever imagine." Victor wrapped his arms around my waist. I immediately looked around to make sure my dad wasn't lurking around. Once I felt the coast was clear I slowly wrapped my arms around his waist and told him "I can't believe you're here. My dad is super protective of me. I can't believe he bought me such a nice car. I could imagine him telling the car salesman to find me the most collision protective unattractive vehicle on the lot. My dad doesn't usually do stuff like this. He was so sad when I told him I was applying to out of state colleges. You know. I'm kind of all he has," I said to him with my arms nestled around his waist, his manhood pressed against my thigh.

"I hope you don't mind me crashing your party. I was with your dad when he was looking at cars for you. He was looking at a Grey Ford Taurus and I told him you looked like a Mustang convertible kind of girl. He was stuck on getting something safe on the road I told him he can't stop fate. The truth is I thought you would look good topless" he said winking at me. "I wanted to see the look on your face when you saw the car", he admitted. He had all of my attention and under the glow of the flood lights over the balcony, I stared into the light in his brown eyes. He raised my chin up towards his, staring into my eyes and I leaned in to kiss him, inhaling the scent of his cologne until our lips met. The fullness of his lips against my glossy lips generated a warm wave inside of me. I quickly pulled away, looking over my shoulders, unsure of where my dad was. I looked up into Victor's eyes wondering if he would kiss me again. But, he didn't kiss me again. Instead he said "Hey, it was good to see you I've got to head out." He brought me close to him. I hugged him tight as he inhaled the scent of my hair and said, "See you later". He got into his black Mercedes Benz and backed out of the driveway and took off. I walked over and sat in my new car inhaling the smell of new leather, still feeling Victor's full juicy lips against mine. I looked over at the passenger seat and saw the unopened purple birthday card from Victor and I opened it.

Londyn,

Happy Birthday! You're a woman now. I want to see you tonight. I'll be at the Stanford Hotel room #526 The Laurel Room.

I couldn't believe that's what was inside the card. It was like it was meant to be. He wrote that card before he got here which meant he was thinking of me and that I kissed him first. This made me know for sure that would be the night that I lost my virginity. I was more excited about seeing him and stepping into my adulthood than I was about my own birthday. But I was ready to step into womanhood. I wanted Victor to be my first. I went inside the house where my dad had cleaned up and had retired to his room for the night. Aunt Gigi had gone to her part of the house so she could lay down. I took a shower and changed my clothes into something easy to remove. I put on a short yellow spring dress, a pair of strappy sandals and pulled my hair back in a ponytail. I yelled upstairs to let my dad know I was leaving the house. The lack of response let me know he was already sleep.

I grabbed my keys and headed to The Stanford Hotel. I was nervous about having sex for the first time. Most of the girls at St. Bernadette's were not virgins, including Angie and Joanna. And most stories were not pleasant and made sex seem troublesome and painful. Angie's first time was in her boyfriend's bedroom with his little brother trying to get in the locked room that they shared. Right as her boyfriend was cumming his little brother busted into the room and she jumped resulting in him bending his dick and having to go to the emergency room. Joanna's first took them to the woods near his house where he'd laid down a bedsheet and brought beer and sandwiches for them to have a picnic on their date. She thought the gesture was so thoughtful and she gave him her flower out there with mother nature. What they didn't know was they were laying on top of and surrounded by poison ivy. They both broke out in itchy hives and blisters and had to explain to their parents why they both had it. I wasn't letting all that discourage me. Being that he was older and experienced, I knew with Victor it would be special.

When I arrived at the Stanford hotel I took the elevator right up to his room. I was nervous as I rode the elevator up five floors. I didn't know how things would start I just knew how I wanted it to end. I walked towards the rooms recognizing each room was named and numbered, counting by twos until I approached room number 526 The Laurel Room at the end of the hallway. Trying not to lose my nerve I took a deep breath and knocked on the door. I thought I heard something in the room, but nobody came to the door. I knocked on the door again, anxiously waiting for the door to open. This time I realized the noise from the room was coming from the room next door, room 524 The Cherry Room. I waited a few minutes until it was evident that no one was in the hotel room. I didn't have his phone number and after waiting a few more agonizing minutes I walked to my car in disappointment. I waited around for about twenty minutes hoping he was just running late, and I could still catch him pulling up, but he didn't come. I went home and wrote in my journal and cried.

The next day was bright and sunny, the light from my bedroom windows poured into my room. I woke up with a headache and puffy eyes. When I woke up I instantly remembered what didn't happen the night before. I was not in the mood to go to work but I never called out and I needed the distraction from my thoughts about Victor. I drove to work in my new mustang convertible and proudly parked her in the employee parking lot with her new temp tag on the rear bumper. It was a Saturday and instead of being in my school uniform I was wearing my yellow short sleeved uniform shirt and black pants that fit snug around my wide hips. I began my shift of spritzing passing customers with my tester bottle of a new fragrance that we were advertising. It was a sweet blend of coriander, rose and musk. The fragrance was a hit, I quickly made my sales quota. I was handing a customer her merchandise in a small yellow paper bag, with Taylor's printed in cursive on the bag, when he suddenly approached me at the counter.

Victor walked up to me at the perfume counter and placed his hand on mine without saying a word. I quickly pulled my hand away.

I didn't have anything to say to him. I ignored him, as if he wasn't standing right there. After a while he broke the silence. "I know I deserve that. I'm sorry. I thought about everything on my way there and I couldn't help but think about your mother's dying wish for you to go to college. You are so close to fulfilling that dream. I don't want to get in the way" he admitted.

"That's not for you to decide" I said trying to show him I'm a woman.

"And, my wife kept questioning where I was going since I hadn't been home all day," he replied.

"Oh, and what did you tell your wife?" I asked rudely.

"I didn't know what to tell her. I guess I didn't plan that out very well," he admitted. "I just wanted to see you." He smiled at me and that broke down my barrier. Being with him made it easier not to be mad at him. I'd cried over him all night and I told myself that I never wanted to see him again, but now that I was with him again I wanted him as much as I could have him. I sprayed my wrist with the new perfume, and I raised my hand to his nose. "Do you like that?" I asked him, fanning my wrist under his nose. "Yes, that smells familiar what is that?" he asked intrigued. "It's the perfume I'm wearing. Buy this for your wife so when you come home smelling like me you're smelling like her."

"OK, ring up the biggest bottle you have. What time do you get off?" he asked me.

"We close at ten", I replied.

"I'll meet you when you get off", he said to me handing me his platinum American Express credit card to pay for his wife's perfume.

He hung out at the perfume counter talking to me for a while until Sheila came out of no where and tried to flirt with him. She walked over to the perfume counter dramatically swinging her hips and being giggly for no reason. He backed away from her and I just laughed. He left and all night she couldn't stop talking about how fine he was and what she would do to him if she saw him again. I allowed her to enjoy her fantasies about him and I continued working the sales floor and I enjoyed fantasies of my own about him.

The end of my shift came quickly, and I was anxious because Victor said he would see me after I got off work, but he didn't tell me where and I still didn't have his phone number. I rode down the escalator in the empty store, as all the lights in the store were being turned off and I walked through the side door out to the dark employee parking lot. Parked next to my new Mustang was a black Mercedes Benz with Victor leaning against it. My co-worker, Sheila saw Victor leaning on my car, recognizing him from her advances and she smirked as she entered her car and quickly pulled away.

Once I was within arm's reach he pulled me to him and kissed me. "I've been waiting all day to kiss you again," he whispered to me. "You would have gotten a lot more than that last night" I confessed before I kissed him with my eyes closed and my body pressed to his, like he was my man. I felt that phantom tingle throughout my body. He held me tight and when I was in his arms nothing else mattered.

We snuck around like that for a few weeks. Most nights when I got off work he was waiting for me in the employee parking lot, where we would spend our time together making out in my car. He still hadn't given me his phone number and I never asked. I just expected him to be there like he said he would, and he was. If he couldn't come he would tell me so I wouldn't be looking for him. When he said he would be there he was and with gifts. One day he overheard me admiring a customer's pandora bracelet as I was trying to make a sale. Her bracelet was full of colorful charms and she shared that there was a story behind each charm, I thought that was special.

The next time he saw me he met me at my car and handed me a jewelry box. I knew he wasn't asking me to marry him, I but still wondered what was inside the small black and white box. To my surprise he was paying attention to what I liked, and he bought me my own Pandora bracelet. The first charm he ever gave me was my favorite. It was a silver charm with pink rhinestone lips. Almost every time he came to see me he brought me a new Pandora charm. Each charm was given with some significance to our romance. Hence why the first charm he ever gave me was my favorite to remember our first kiss. That was followed by a heart charm then a rose charm and then he gave me a perfume charm. Until I had seen him so much that my charm bracelet was already full. I wore my bracelet every day and I never took it off. He was beginning to come to my job so often the other employees would ask about him. Then we would find random secretive places to meet to be more discreet. I was spending so much time with Victor after work I wasn't leaving much time to study. I got a C on an exam and I freaked out. I couldn't remember ever getting below a B before. I told him about my grade and he too was disappointed that our relationship was affecting me at school.

CHAPTER EIGHT

The next time I saw him we were sitting in my car kissing and talking about how much we wanted to be with each other when he got a call on his large cell phone. It was his wife looking for him. He looked at me when he answered the phone, motioning his finger to his mouth so I would remain quiet and said, "I'm out with a very important client and I will have to call you back" and he abruptly hung up the phone. I couldn't believe he did that. I didn't know how to feel. I was flattered that he blew off his wife for me, but he also looked me dead in the eye and referred to me as his client. I wanted him to call me his woman. I watched him put his phone on silent as it buzzed in his pants over and over again as she called back to back. He told me he wouldn't be around for a while so he could allow things to cool off. He tried to sell me on our cool off time was mostly to keep my dad under the radar, but I know it was mostly due to his wife. I hated that I wanted him so bad. So many things about this was wrong. He was my dad's colleague much older than me and most importantly he was married. I told him to get out of my car and I never wanted to see him again. He begged me to reason with him, but I just couldn't. I was developing very strong feelings for him and I knew I would be the one hurt in the end because, of course there would be an end to this. I was barely legal. I knew it was wrong to want him, but I didn't stop him as he leaned over the center console and slid his arm around me pulling me close to him. His hands gripped my thighs by the handful under my romper, his hands made their way to the center of my thighs. He kissed me and slowly pulled my panties to the side, his finger sliding inside my juicy girl pond. He touched something that's never been felt by anyone else before and I thrust myself into the palm of his hand. I leaned back to spread my legs wider until my left thigh was pressed against the door handle and the seatbelt latch imprinted into my right thigh. He pulled his fingers from between my thighs and suck the creamy juice from his fingers and then inserts them back inside of me. He used his thumb to rub circles around my clit, as his fingers explored my warm pussy that was tingling from every angle. I felt my body approaching a feeling I'd never felt before, but it was coming so fast I couldn't stop it from happening. It felt like when you sit too long, and your foot goes to sleep but all over your body starting from your clit. I experienced an orgasm for the first time that was not self-inflicted. I looked down and his dick was rock hard in his creased slacks. "You're beautiful" he said to me. He leaned over to me with his juicy lips pressed against mine, sliding my tongue against his. I sat back and began putting my clothes back together when his phone began buzzing again. He ignored it for the first few rings. "If I don't answer she's just going to keep calling," he declared. He sat back in the passenger seat and answered his wife, responding that he was on the way home. I heard her tell him to pick up the baby's medication from the pharmacy before they closed. I never knew he had a child. "alright I got it" he said. "I'll be home soon" he told his wife and hung up his cell phone. I looked up at him surprised "When were you going to tell me, you had a baby?"

"I didn't lie about my son, we never talked about children," he said. "What do you want to know about him" he asked me abruptly? I rolled my eyes at him and asked, "what is his name...how old is he?", with an attitude.

"His name is Noah, he is two years old and yes he is my only child." I still couldn't believe I was sneaking around with a married man with a baby at home. "Victor, I can't do this with you. You have a whole family at home. There's nothing here for me." Tears slowly began to tread down my face. "I don't want to see you anymore. Please get out of my car," I said politely. He tried to plead with me, but I was not hearing it. I began to scream at him "Get out of my car, get out of my car!"

He got out of the car and sat in his car with the engine running, looking at me through the side window for a few minutes. I just sat there avoiding making eye contact. He finally pulled off and I balled my eyes out in my car alone in the dark empty parking lot.

As the weeks went on I was involved in many of the senior activities so during this time, it was easy to avoid him. I was trying to forget about Victor and continued to go to school and work. One day as I was standing in the aisle with my tester fragrance I looked up and recognized Lisa Crawford, Victor's wife approaching me. I was unsure what to do because she was fast-approaching me. I just stood there holding my tester bottle trying to seem normal, but I was nervous and sweating and unsure of what to do next.

"Hi, you're the little girl from the Christmas party right?", she asked.

Here we go with that little girl shit again, I thought but I just nodded my head in agreeance.

"Londyn", I clarified.

"Oh, I didn't know you worked here. Can you tell me where the lingerie section is?", she inquired looking around at the store signs hanging from the ceiling. "It's my anniversary and my husband is taking me on a trip to Jamaica", she said smiling as I pointed towards the lingerie department. Having to interact with his wife was nerve wrecking. I just knew that she knew and that's why she wanted to approach me. I hadn't seen Victor in a few weeks and at the moment I was glad I called it off with him. Had I not, there's a good chance he could have been there with me when she walked over since he liked to pop up on me at work and hang out with me around the perfume counter. I was so relieved that she wasn't approaching me about being with her husband as my racing heart slowed down. My eyes followed her around until I saw her check out and leave the store. That experience reminded me that I needed to forget about Victor. I finished my shift and went home to write my feelings into my journal, talk to my friends on the phone and get some sleep.

Over the next few days I was busy getting ready for prom and studying for finals and Victor was busy with family or business I presumed. Although I must admit that upon leaving work I would anxiously walk to my car hoping Victor would be there leaning against my car waiting for me. He wasn't there but I couldn't stop thinking about him. Every time I closed my eyes I wanted to feel him again, but I knew I couldn't.

CHAPTER NINE

It was the week of the senior prom and everything was feeling normal, other than I was still heartbroken over Victor. Then I got a call from Joanna, that shaded my new normal. She called me at the beginning of the week to tell me the boy I'd had a crush on since ninth grade, Anthony, at the last minute asked her to the prom and she said she'd go with him. I never told her I had a crush on him, and I never even spoke to him after he laughed at me in my granny bra, so how could I be mad that he asked her to the prom, but I was. At that point I had no date to my senior prom, which was just days away. Angie was going with her boyfriend Ryan and now Joanna was going with Anthony. I suddenly no longer wanted to go to the prom but was it too late to get out of going, I thought? I would be the only lonely one there and I was already feeling down and in no shape to deal with that too.

My aunt Gigi never had any children, I was like the daughter she never had, so it was a big deal for her to get me ready for my prom and I didn't know how to tell her I didn't want to go. In the weeks leading up to the prom Aunt Gigi had taken me dress shopping and shoe shopping and shared with me the story of how she helped get my mom ready for her prom with my dad.

This occasion meant so much to her, I still didn't know how to tell her that I didn't want to go. Prom was on a Friday so I thought maybe I could find a date by then.

The day of prom I left school and went straight home where my aunt Gigi had the glam squad ready to make me feel like Cinderella. I was in the middle of getting my makeup applied when tears began to drop from my eyes one at a time thinking about how lonely I was going to feel. My aunt Gigi saw me crying and I told her that I didn't have a date and that I didn't want to go but I didn't know how to tell her because it meant so much to her. She hugged me and told me not to worry. "Your aunt Gigi got you" she said telling the glam squad to keep getting me ready as she walked out of my bedroom door.

Aunt Gigi walked downstairs to my dad's office where he seemed to be on an important call that she didn't want to interrupt, and she quietly walked in and sat in an empty chair, until she could get his attention.

"Hold on a sec", my dad moved the phone from his ear, looking at my Aunt Gigi. "Is she ready to go already?", he questioned.

"No, her friend bailed on her and is going with a date and now she doesn't want to go because she'll be solo. What are we going to do? She seems dead set against going", my aunt informed my dad.

"You go back there and make sure she'll be the most beautiful girl at that prom, and I'll think of something", he demanded.

My aunt trusted my dad would figure something out and came back in my room with me where my hair was being wand curled.

Meanwhile my dad was on the phone telling his colleague about my troubles. My aunt didn't know it was Victor on the other end of the phone who she just made aware of my teenage crisis. Victor offered my dad a solution. Victor offered to get his nephew Jason to be my prom date. Jason graduated from another local high school the year before and was living at home while working at the airport. My dad didn't like the idea of me going out with someone he didn't know, and he immediately turned that idea down.

"Elton, at least you don't have to worry about her with no knucklehead trying to harm her. My nephew is around her age and he's a good kid," he assured. "My sister was a single mom and I raised that kid like he was my son," Victor explained. Elton seemed skeptical about this plan. "It's done. I just text my nephew and he said ok." Victor told my dad he just needed an hour and Jason would be there. My dad reluctantly agreed and ended the call. He then came into my room admiring the resemblance to my mom's prom dress. I chose a more modern version of her vanilla lace, floor length dress. My dress was white, spaghetti strapped and fitted to my body showing off my curves. It plunged down the back exposing my brown skin to the base of my round ass and my ample cleavage seen through a flesh tone mesh in the front, that traveled to the navel of the dress. Everyone in the glam squad was admiring me in my dress, trying to hype me up about going and having a good time and reminiscing about their own prom experiences. I kept telling dad and Aunt Gigi that I didn't want to go, but they insisted they'd worked it out. I didn't know what *worked it out meant*, but I reluctantly went along. Aunt Gigi was ready to take my picture. I was standing in the foyer posing for my photo op near a picture of my mother hanging on the wall, next to my mother's porcelain urn, when I heard the sound of a car engine pull up in the driveway. I picked up my floor length gown from the bottom and I began to walk over to the window. I looked out and I saw a black stretch Cadillac Escalade parking in the horseshoe driveway. Aunt Gigi yelled, "Come in". I walked towards the front door, abruptly stopping mid step, my heart was racing, the moment felt surreal. In walked this strange boy. He walked in my front door holding a red and white corsage, matching his red pocket square in his black tuxedo.

"Who are you?" I questioned.

"You must be Londyn," he said, I was surprised he knew my name. "I'm Jason, I graduated from Frederick Douglass High last year. I'm here to take you to your prom"

"Are you serious?" I whispered to him. I couldn't believe this was happening. He walked over to me amazed at how gorgeous I looked, by the "Wow" he exhaled, and he placed the corsage of red and white carnations and baby's breath around my wrist.

I couldn't believe my dad was okay with me going out with a strange guy. But, I thought if my dad was ok with it than this guy must be ok. Jason winked at me gesturing his arm to me and he walked me to the car reassuring my dad he would have me home at a decent time.

"Hey, you respect my niece", my aunt Gigi inserted.

The car smelled of expensive cologne and leather, the driver's privacy shield up right. Inside the car we sat next to one another as we were driven to the venue. This year prom was being held at the Marriott Marquis in Downtown Atlanta and we were just a short drive away. That was the longest, short ride coming from my house in Buckhead. At first I wasn't sure what to say, he just stared at me in silence, like he was having a conversation with me in his head, so I blurted something out just to break the ice. "I don't know what my dad told you, but I hope you're not doing this out of pity. I don't need you to feel sorry for me. This was not my idea," I quickly informed him.

Suddenly I realized we'd arrived at the prom; the driver exited and came to open my door. To my unconscionable surprise Victor was standing there in a tuxedo holding my door open. I exited the car and Jason exited behind me.

"This was my idea", Victor said admiring how glamorous and grown up I looked. "I haven't been able to get you out of my head. I've missed you. I wasn't sure how I would see you again so, I jumped at the opportunity to see you tonight", he said to me before he leaned in to kiss me.

"Alright, Unc," Jason said as I questioned if he meant Unc as in uncle.

"I'll be back to pick y'all up when it's over just hit me up" Jason said walking around to get in the driver's seat.

I quickly got myself together and reapplied my red lipstick. He wiped the ruby tint from his lips with his pocket square and put his arm around me to escort me inside. As he admired the corsage on my right wrist he noticed I was still wearing my pandora bracelet. Before walking through the doors to go inside I leaned into him and asked him what about his wife. His response gave me chills. He told me "I'm all yours tonight." We walked into the cool hotel lobby and I gave my name to a girl on the prom committee to cross my name off the list. Once we had our wrist bands on we walked over to the photographer to take our photo. I wasn't sure how to get out of taking the photo and before I knew it we were standing on the black x on the floor, taking the traditional couple's photo, with Victor standing behind me with his arms around my waist showing off the corsage. We embraced one another, smiling as if we were really a couple. We then rode down the escalator where the sound of the music grew louder and louder. The familiar beat of Little John and the East Side Boys filled the air downstairs. The prom theme was Enchanted Nights. We walked into the strobing white lights and I searched through the crowd of young familiar faces, looking for Angie, Joanna and their dates. I spotted them sitting at a round decorated table in the back of the ball room. Angie saw us and waved us down, she recognized Victor from my birthday party. I wasn't sure how the night would go. I forgot that I had been mad at him. We actually had a great time together, the six of us laughed and we danced all night. He was super cool around my friends and nobody even mentioned the apparent age difference. Before the end of the night Victor and I went into the photobooth and took a strip of four photos with me sitting on his lap. I hid the photos in my purse. My besties swore to keep my prom date swap a secret and to hide the photos.

At the end of the night I asked Victor if he would come back to my room when he dropped me off. He hesitated, afraid of being caught by my dad, until I told him there's a way to sneak into my room by coming in through the kitchen entrance and walking up the back steps. When we pulled up to the house I was straddling his lap in the limo seat with my dress hiked up, kissing him passionately. He told his nephew to cut off the engine but be ready to go at any minute.

"Watch for my signal when I get up to my room I'll flash the lights once if it's ok to come up and twice if you need to go" I said to him. I kissed him as I exited the car with my heels in my hand.

I quietly walked in first to make sure the coast was clear. I walked by my dad's room to make sure he was sleep and I heard him snoring with the door closed. Once I got in my bedroom I flashed the lights one time to let Victor know he could come up to my room. He made his way to my room and I let him in. He was amazed by being in my bedroom and learning more about me. He walked around looking at the posters of my favorite celebrities and family pictures that were hung on the walls and mirrors. He began to walk around admiring my ballet trophies from when I was a little girl. Not many people knew at one point I wanted to be a prima ballerina. After a few minutes I asked him if he wouldn't mind unzipping me from my dress. He removed his jacket and threw it over the vanity chair, and he stood behind me and slowly pulled the zipper down from my dress. His hands removed my dress from my shoulders, exposing my bare breasts and nude thong panties. Victor stood there admiring every inch of my body. He took his warm hands and cupped my breasts, his thumbs rubbing circles around the darkest part of them. He leaned down and with his mouth he began to caress my firm nipples with his tongue dancing in circles. He walked me over to my bed, laid me down on top of my pink floral comforter still admiring my body. He unbuttoned his shirt and I kissed him pulling him on top of me with only my panties on. His dick was hard pressed against my stomach, I could feel his hardness through his pants. My legs wrapped around him, his body covered mine and we grinded each other like he was inside of me. I knew the moment I was waiting for was approaching. He was still fully clothed, I only had my panties on, I wanted him to know that I was ready for him to go all the way. I took my panties off and dropped them on the floor beside the bed. I continued to kiss him rubbing my clit against his hard manhood through his pants.

He pulled his lips away from mine and began to kiss my neck, slightly biting my skin. He then reunited his lips with my exposed nipples and continued to kiss my soft naked body, parting my virgin lips with his tongue, I leaned all the way back on to the bed. I stared at the ceiling, counting the sparkles in the stucco, trying not to be loud as he sucked the young soul out of my pussy. I wrapped my legs around his neck and put a pillow over my face when I started to feel that phantom tingle travel through my body. That's when I heard my dad walking down the hall. I scrambled to my feet and I whispered for Victor to hurry up and get in the bathroom and I tossed him his tuxedo jacket from the vanity chair.

I threw on my robe and opened my bedroom door for my dad who just wanted to hear how the prom went. "Hey baby girl. How was your night?" he asked curiously looking around.

"Prom was great dad!" I nervously exclaimed. "I had a really great time," I said looking around the room for any evidence of Victor.

"That's good. He was a gentleman right?," he questioned.

"Who Jason?" I asked to clarify. I reassuringly answered my dad. "Yes, my cherry is still safe dad. No worries dad. I'm not interested in Victor's nephew", I laughed.

"I didn't ask but since you shared, very good. I'm glad to hear you had a great time and that things are how they should be" he said proudly. My dad left my room and Victor walked out of the bathroom with a stunned look on his face.

"Londyn did I hear you right? You're a virgin?" he said looking surprised.

 "Yes so. What's it to you?", I said with an attitude.

"If your dad hadn't come in I don't know how far we would have gone," he admitted, "but I don't know if I can be the man who takes your virginity. I'm already starting to fall in love with you without that adding to how I feel." I held onto his words that he was falling in love with me and I leaned in for a kiss. He kissed me back as if my dad wasn't just seconds down the hall, but then he pulled away. "There's so many reasons why this can't happen", he began to stutter. "I'm married, I have a family, you're my boss's daughter and you're only eighteen", he admitted.

"I know but I want you", I said kissing him intensely making him take a step back as he opened my robe and slid his hands over my firm, round ass. He told me he had to leave before my dad saw the Escalade still parked in the driveway. He kissed me and told me he would see me soon. A few minutes later I heard the car pull off and I was left to writing about the night in my journal. I took the photo that we took in the photobooth and placed it inside my journal and tucked my pink notebook inside my floral pillow case on top of by bed. After laying in my bed dreaming about what almost happened again, I eventually fell asleep with the intoxicating scent of Victor's cologne still in my bed comforter.

CHAPTER TEN

Victor came to see me the next weekend, while I was working my perfume counter. He asked me out so we could spend some time together. I was excited to see him, I really missed him, and I decided that I wanted to spend as much time with him as I could, before I would be leaving for college and I agreed to meet him. I later found out my dad was hosting some mandatory business dinner on the same night I was supposed to be meeting up with Victor. I heard him on the phone with my dad trying to get out of it, but my dad wouldn't hear it, so that meant our plans were cancelled. I overheard my dad finalizing the meeting plans with Victor. They planned to have the meeting at Josephine's Bistro, a chic new lounge in midtown. I thought business meetings were boring, but because I wanted to see Victor that night I told my dad I would be his escort to that meeting. My dad agreed to let me accompany him and I got dressed to impress. I arrived on my father's arm, walking into a room with men in suits and their prudish wives. I approached the long, elegantly dressed dinner table and saw Victor sitting next to a beautiful woman in a short black cocktail dress. I recognized her from the Christmas party. Unlike at the Christmas party where I chose to observe them all night, this time I was forced to sit and watch him smile at her and touch her throughout the dinner. I watched all night, wanting to replace her with me. I admired her hands observing the enormous rock on her finger. He must really love her, I thought. What did I get myself into, I questioned?

After feeling tortured through dinner, I waited until his wife walked away to the ladies' room and I approached him. I told him to ditch his wife and meet me in the employee parking lot of Taylor's department store and he better not stand me up. I walked away just as his wife was headed towards us. I then smirked as I overheard him tell his wife how the dinner is boring, and they probably wouldn't stay long. She on the other hand was enjoying the night out away from the baby and she wanted to stay. He was adamant about leaving causing an argument between them. I witnessed the escalation from across the room with a devious smile. Once I saw him and his wife angrily leave I told my dad I was going to meet up with the girls and I kissed him good night. I asked my dad's driver to take me home. There I blew through my bedroom changing my clothes and shoes and I jumped into my car to meet Victor. Part of me knew it was a long shot that he would be there and that I really shouldn't get my hopes up. But I did. My expectations were way up there, and I was going to be absolutely devastated if he didn't come. I drove through the mall entrance and straight to the side of Taylor's department store. It was late, the overhead lights disturbed the darkness of the vacant parking lot. As I approached the dark employee parking lot I saw a single car parked. Victor was sitting in his car, with the headlights off. I pulled up beside him and walked around to sit on his passenger side. Once seated, I pulled the door closed and I leaned over and pulled him to me, wrapping my hands around his neck and my lips around his. I felt like I wasn't complete until I had him. "I don't know what you've done to me", he whispered, grazing my lips as he spoke. I took the lever on the side of the seat and pushed him as far back as the seat could reach, leaving him staring at the roof. I leaned over him lost in the rhythm of our kiss. I opened my eyes to see the excitement in his face as he fought the urge to make love to me. I began to aggressively unzip his pants and remove his belt. I freed his manhood observing that it was everything I expected it to be. He was long, slightly hung to the right and it wasn't ugly. I surprised him when he felt me lean over him, taking all of him into my warm mouth. My mouth dripping with spit anxiously awaiting his entry. I didn't know what he was expecting but I know he wasn't expecting that. He moaned and jolted back in pleasure. I could feel he was unsure how aggressive to be with me. Maybe his wife liked it soft. I took his hand placed it on the back of my head and bobbed my head up and down, in a mechanical motion, trying to remember what I learned from watching my dad's porn. Profanity began to leave his mouth, so I knew I was doing something right. This was the first time I ever gave oral sex. I closed my eyes and I continued to slurp on him until he couldn't handle it anymore and he exploded in my mouth. I couldn't believe what just happened. Was I still a virgin, I thought? Well my mouth wasn't. Victor began to put his pants back on as I wiped his DNA from my mouth with a napkin I found in the glove box. I kissed him one more time and said, "I want you so bad" and I exited his car and sped off in mine. I went home and wrote in my journal. While sitting up with my bed with my journal in my lap, Angie called me and said she and Joanna were in the neighborhood and wanted to come over and crash for the night. I welcomed them over for some girl time. It would be one of the last times I would see them before we parted for college. After the girls came over I couldn't keep it to myself and I told them about my relationship with Victor.

"I already knew something was going on when I saw him at your party", Angie said. "It was like he saw no one else in the room but you. I saw how your poor aunt was trying to push up on him too," she laughed.

"He didn't pay her any attention, all he saw was you", Joanna chimed in. "I mean, I knew something was going on when I saw him at prom. Londyn, I've known you for four years and I've never seen you like this about anyone. You love this man, girl", she said to me. I shook my head at her denying the accusation. We spent the rest of the night sharing stories of going all the way and almost going all the way.

CHAPTER ELEVEN

The next time I saw Victor he appeared at my graduation party. He played the role of the father's supportive colleague with my friends gawking in the background, they almost gave us away. Graduation was emotional as I watched all the students hugging their moms. I'd worked so hard to achieve academic excellence. I was our class salutatorian and proudly walked across the stage having earned my high school diploma after being accepted to the college of my dreams on a scholarship..

When the ceremony was over I walked over to meet my family and Victor was there standing with them. Just like my birthday he gave me a purple card. When I motioned to open it, he pushed my hand down and he told me to open it when I got in the car and then he said he had to go. I was headed to my favorite restaurant to enjoy my graduation dinner with my family and friends. I would be leaving them in eight weeks, at the end of the summer to head to Philadelphia. Once alone in the car I opened the card. Written on the card was a note.

Londyn,

*I miss you and I want a do over. Meet me at The
Stanford hotel Room 526, The Laurel Room
tonight!*

Was he serious, I thought? Certainly, he didn't think
I was going to come running up to his hotel room
just to be humiliated again. I went to my graduation
dinner enjoying making memories but at the same
time thinking about Victor's invitation to meet him in
his hotel room. Against my better judgment, after
attending my graduation party with my family I left to
meet Victor for a private party of our own. This time
when I arrived at the room he was there to greet me.

He kissed me as he greeted me at the door. I walked
into the room for the first time, admiring the décor
and how romantic it felt. The room was much bigger
than I expected. He had roses all over the room and
rose petals sprinkled across the king size bed. I
recognized the label on the vase and then I knew the
Valentine's Day flowers were from him. That made
me want him even more than before. There was a
half empty glass of scotch on the bar that he picked
up to finish as I walked around the room. I observed
there were very thick red curtains drawn together in
the room. They reminded me of the velvet red
curtains at the theatre where my dad would take me
to see the Nut Cracker every Christmas. I excused
myself to the bathroom to freshen up and changed
into something that would turn him on. I decided I'd
put on a show for him. That night I allowed Victor to

explore parts of me that no one had ever experienced before. He was gentle as he caressed my body in my red lingerie. He walked me over to the bed and laid me on my stomach as he massaged my soft, thick thighs. He leaned down kissing my bottom cheeks, sending chills up and down my spine. He gently flipped me over onto my back and he slowly slid the red lace nightie down my thighs with his mouth, leaving me laying there naked on the bed while he removed his clothes. I laid there admiring his perfect body, as he undressed, my eyes glued to his hard dick. I wanted him inside of me and I parted my thighs to let him know I was ready. He tasted me first. He had me wetter than a sailor's path. Then he kissed every part of my body and then leaned over to the nightstand, tore open a gold condom wrapper with his teeth and put on the only thing between us. Then he leaned over me, his hard dick probing at the entrance of my moistness, looking me in my eyes for one more moment of reassurance. I opened my legs wider to let him know I was ready. He slowly entered me, I shuttered in shock. It was the best worst feeling of my life. It was a pleasurable pain and I did not want him to stop. He slowly stroked inside of me, his sweating body on top of mine, kissing my lips with our fingers intertwined, my head pressed against the pillow. When I felt that phantom tingle I pressed my palms into his back, pushing him deeper inside of me until he couldn't take it anymore. Afterwards, we laid there in silence, maybe we were in disbelief. He asked me how I was feeling, and I told him it was the best day of my life. We made love again that night and the next time it didn't hurt so bad. The next morning, I woke up in the bed in Victor's arms. My young pussy was sore from inexperience. We didn't have to check out until noon, so I leaned over Victor's sleeping body and used my tongue to guide his soft dick in my mouth, until he was nice and hard and fully awake. I sat on top of him and guided him inside of me. We made love again until it was time to check out.

I drove home in my new Mustang ready to sneak in the house prepared to use the excuse that I was with Angie all night. I pulled up to my house and saw my dad was gone. I completely forgot he told me he and Aunt Gigi had to fly out right after graduation, on business. My aunt Gigi had become like my dad's personal stylist as he traveled for various meetings and appearances. I walked into my empty house, past my mother's urn and went up to my room. I jumped in the shower, washing away Victor's scent from my body, thinking about all the emotions from my night with Victor. Once out of the shower, I threw on my house dress, I picked up my journal and began to write about my first time when I heard my door bell ring. I put my journal and pen down on the bed I rushed to answer the front door. To my surprise it was Victor at the door. I opened the front door and asked what he was doing there? He picked me up and carried me to my bedroom. He laid me on my bed, knocking the journal on the carpet and lifted up my dress. He was pleased to see that I didn't have any panties on. He bent me over the bed, my hands gripped the pink comforter as he plunged face first into my wetness. With my juiciness dripping from his chin he quickly pulled a condom from his pocket and stroked me deep and hard, my ass slapping against his thighs as I forced my knees to grip the comforter. We made love over and over again. I'd never done drugs, but I felt like I was on a sexual high.

He admitted that my dad called him from the airport and told him that he'd be back in a few days and to look out for me. Victor told his wife he was on a business trip with my dad and he stayed at the house with me for the next few days making love to me again and again. I'd fallen in love with Victor, there was no denying it. My body craved his. For the rest of the summer I spent my time hanging out with my besties before we split up to go off to college and sneaking off with Victor.

CHAPTER TWELVE

Towards the end of that incredibly hot Georgia summer I quit my job at Taylor's department store as I prepared to leave for The University of Pennsylvania. I was so excited about going to college. I couldn't wait to be independent and from under my father's scrutiny. I had mixed emotions about leaving Victor.

The closer it got to me leaving for college the more Victor came around. He would find reasons to come around the house to meet with my dad and find more discreet locations where we could be together. Sometimes we'd meet up in the middle of the day, drive to the top of Arabian mountain and have sex in the backseat of my Mustang. Before I left for college I met up with Victor one last time at the Stanford hotel. He fucked me like he knew it would be our last time together. He promised me he would come visit me at my dorm and he assured me that he loved me, and he would find a way for us to be together. I believed him. He had a part of my heart that no man could ever have. We made love again in the same room where I lost my virginity, until I finally had to leave. I kissed him good-bye and left him laying naked in the hotel room. I had no clue what was going to happen next with us.

I departed the next day to head to Pennsylvania, my dad and Aunt Gigi drove me there with all of my stuff packed in the car. I had to leave my car in Georgia since freshman couldn't drive.

I thought about my mom the entire trip. Looking out the window at the thousands of trees flowing along the interstate I smiled knowing she was watching her dream happen. She would have loved to be on that trip with us. I felt her, like when I walked across the stage as I was handed my diploma.

It took us fifteen hours to drive there between bathroom breaks, food breaks, gas fill ups and stretch breaks because my dad's joints would start to hurt. When we pulled up to the historic brick building I felt like I was walking in the footsteps of a celebrity. I noticed the guys on campus already checking me out. My dad noticed too, mean mugging any young man that looked my way. I moved into my mother's old dorm, on the third floor. My mom was a resident advisor for the dorm when she was a student. Her room was by the snack machine that was still there filled with the same generic chips, fruit snacks, chocolate and sodas. I immediately felt my mom's presence with me as I entered my door room.

I remember it was a hot, beautiful day in late August, almost as hot as it was back in Georgia. It was the first day all the incoming freshman could arrive and there were lots of young students and families moving around the large campus. It was funny

watching dad and Aunt Gigi struggle to carry my
heavy totes up three flights of stairs. Once everything
was upstairs they had to sit down on my bare twin
size bed, their chests panting out of breath, they both
complained their backs hurt. Shortly after I was
settled in my dorm room dad's phone rang. It was
Victor on the other end. I could hear him say he just
wanted to make sure we made it safely. I yelled
through the phone, "You know...my dad almost
killed us trying to avoid traffic in Washington D.C.",
I laughed. My dad instantly denied it, but Aunt Gigi
chimed in, "Mmmhmm, he almost fell asleep at the
wheel, talking about he was just blinking his eyes." I
snatched the cell phone away from my dad and
spoke to Victor directly. "Don't believe him he's
getting old", I teased. I nonchalantly walked out of
the cluttered dorm room and down to the other end
of the hall so I could talk to Victor in private.
"Victor, I miss you. Why couldn't you come?" I
asked checking to make sure my dad wasn't around.
"I wanted to, but I couldn't" he said.

I made that conversation quick as I looked over my
shoulder for eaves droppers. "Look Victor, I don't
know what we thought was going to happen but we
both know that nothing can come from this. It was
hard enough to see you when we were in the same
city and now I'm hours away. Honestly I just want to
focus on school and enjoy the college experience, so
I think it's best that we just end things now and just
be friends. Victor reluctantly agreed. Dad and Aunt
Gigi left to head back to Atlanta a few hours later

after helping unpack and organize my room, Then I was on my own. On my own, left to my own thoughts. All my thoughts surrounded around Victor and wanting to be with him. It was hard getting over him. Sometimes I would think about quitting school and ending his marriage so we could be together. Then there was the day I saw Victor come across my social media as a friend suggestion. I hesitated for a few minutes before I clicked on his page and began scrolling down his timeline, looking at all the posted photos with his wife and son. His son was getting bigger and more handsome like his father. I also observed a recent photo of his wife where she was visibly pregnant. Did I expect that he wasn't sleeping with his wife while he was fucking me? Seeing this sent me into an emotional cyclone. This just reminded me that he was off limits to me and that he was living his life and I wasn't. I had to let him go. I knew it was best to forget about him and move on. So, I did. I immersed myself into the college life and focused on making my mother proud.

It was a while before I visited home in Atlanta. I didn't want to see Victor or risk running into him. When I did visit from school, I avoided him like the plague. I flew down the for the holidays and eventually drove my car back to school the next summer. I conveniently always had an important school event that I couldn't get out of whenever my dad would invite me to one of his company events. I decided it was best to forget about Victor and move on. I didn't want to see him, and although the memories faded, I never forgot about him.

I got focused on my studies and I was determined to carry out my mother's dying wish and make my family proud. I didn't make much time for a social life and I spent a lot of time in the university library to maintain my four point zero grade point average. It wasn't until the beginning of my senior year in college that I met someone new.

In my final year I met Mike Ramsey, a bio engineer student at the University of Penn, who was planning to enlist in the Navy after graduation. We met one day during homecoming. I thought he was charming and really attractive and super smart. When I first met him, I was sitting on the grass in the middle of the day in between homecoming activities, after the parade and he asked me to share some grass with me. I didn't smoke weed so I told him "No", in disgust. He looked at me and begged, pointing to the ground and that's when I realized he literally wanted to share the grass with me and sit beside me. He was corny like that, but I started to really like him. I hadn't allowed myself to feel that way about anyone since Victor. I hadn't seen or heard from Victor in years and that's how I wanted it, even though I was always surprised how I was able to dodge him when I would go home to Atlanta. I enjoyed being with Mike, he made me feel important and special. Mike was a good man to me. He loved that I was a southern girl and he would often playfully tease me about my southern accent. Mike never knew about my trust fund. We genuinely loved each other, and I never questioned if he was with me because of money.

After four intellectually challenging, uneventful, yet amazing college years the family came to watch me fulfill my mother's dream of having her only daughter graduate from college. I was Valedictorian for my class and graduated with a bachelor's degree in Forensic Accounting from The University of Pennsylvania. I practiced my speech in the mirror and in front of Mike until I had it almost memorized. I wanted my speech to be inspiring and memorable across the generations in attendance. I spoke from the heart and the message was clear. "Live your life on your own terms, appreciate what life's experiences teach you and never allow someone to tell you how to be you." I ended by telling the graduating class, "Remember deductive reasoning is a thing", the audience erupted in laughter, "listen to that voice inside of you, that you can't hide from or lie to," I added as a side note, "and live every day to be the best version of yourself, to be a better you than yesterday so if it were your last day you could say to yourself job well done. Thank you." I made it through my speech, my mouth was so dry, and I was so nervous. As I was projecting through the microphone on the podium, I was trying not to focus on anyone person, but rather feel the energy in the room.

I felt my mother with me as I walked across the lit stage of the auditorium, as I was handed my diploma. I had a picture of me and my mom hugging each other before I went off to my first day of kindergarten printed on a t-shirt under my black gown. I knew she was there with me and I was so happy, tears were slowly streaming from my eyes, because I knew I was making her proud. I also knew that meant I had full access to my inheritance.

 Mike found me through the crowd of black caps and gowns and flagged me over to meet up with him. We hugged in excitement and took a few pictures with some friends. I spotted Dad, Aunt Gigi and Grandma Jean in the lobby looking expensive in their attire. My dad wanted to do the most because my mother would have wanted a big celebration. I advised him that if she were still living she'd know me by now to know that I like to keep it simple. I don't need the party. I'm good with just going out to eat. And after all it is Mike's night too. My boo graduated with his Masters in bio engineering", I added, kissing Mike on the cheek.

My father made dinner plans for the four of us after the graduation. Without asking my dad, I invited Mike to come with us. I could tell he did not agree, but because it was a special night he let me have my way. Against my father's intention, together the five of us went out to dinner after the very long graduation ceremony. This was the first time my dad really saw me with a guy, and I could tell he didn't like it. He still saw me as his baby girl. But, I was twenty-two and I was living my life and I wanted Mike to be the man in my life. My dad was going to have to learn how to deal with it.

CHAPTER THIRTEEN

I knew things between Mike, and I were getting serious. We'd met each other's families, and we'd discussed moving in together after graduation. That's just what we did. Then as planned Mike enlisted in the Army and I was hired with the City of Philadelphia. Although I knew it was coming because I kept seeing lots of his social media likes for jewelry, I was still surprised when he did it. Before he left for bootcamp, as we sat at the small table in our apartment, eating the dinner I'd just heated in the microwave he asked me to marry him. Still chewing and with food in my mouth I said 'yes', and we ran off the next day to the courthouse and got married. We didn't tell anyone. We wanted it to be a surprise.

After we left the courthouse, we stopped and got some takeout Chinese food and we went back to our apartment. Our wedding night was our first time together sexually. I didn't want sex to cloud my judgement or get in the way of me graduating. I couldn't risk getting pregnant. I had to remain focused. The whole no sex thing was usually a deal breaker for most college guys. But, he never pressured me about it or seemed to feel that sex was missing in our relationship. Mike was just the second man I had been with sexually. I began thinking about my first time. It had been so long. Would it feel like the first time, I thought? We really didn't talk about sex much. I don't know how many women Mike was with before me, but I could tell he was inexperienced by the awkward way he moved his body. The entire time, that I laid there I compared him to Victor, and I wasn't satisfied. Sex with Mike felt like a wet fish humping me. Because I loved him I was hopeful that our sex life would get better over time and I faked it.

Mike was from New Jersey and had never been to Georgia and that weekend, for our honeymoon we took a trip to Atlanta. It wasn't much of a honeymoon, but it was a much needed get away. My dad only met Mike once, when we graduated, and I was hoping on this trip they could get to know one another. Mike was down to earth, smart and well mannered, he came from a good family and he adored me. Mike was very intelligent and was entering the military as a high-ranking officer immediately after graduation.

 I wanted Mike to see where I grew up. We decided to surprise my dad and instead of staying at a hotel, I wanted to stay at the house. We caught an early morning flight out of Philly, and we arrived in Atlanta before noon. We drove the rental car into the horseshoe driveway that could use a fresh coat of paint.

"Wow this is the biggest house on the street", Mike said in awe as we approached the front door. We left our luggage in the car and I used my key to let us in.

The house was quiet, except for the noise from the aquarium filter in the foyer. I knocked on my dad's bedroom door and opened it slightly when I didn't hear anything, but I knew he was home because I saw his car in the driveway. I peeked in the door and I couldn't believe what I saw. My dad was asleep in bed with Aunt Gigi. I quietly closed the door and walked into the living room where Mike was sitting on the couch holding the remote flipping through channels looking for something sports related. I was so shocked I couldn't get my words out I was tripping over my tongue. I spoke faster than I ever had before trying to explain what I'd just seen. I tried to figure out the time line of when this happened. My mom died when I was eight and Aunt Gigi was always around. I thought it was admirable of her how she stepped in and cared for me and my dad. Although I had my suspicions over time, I was in disbelief at the thought of them together. After while they woke up and heard that I was home. I would usually call to tell him I'm coming home, but not that time. They were both surprised and caught off guard. My heart started beating rapidly as I heard them walk into the living room. My dad looked like he was ashamed for me to find out. Aunt Gigi wearing her satin nightgown and robe with her short hair tied up, walked up to my dad and slapped him on the back of the head and shouted at him "get a grip Elton, it's been long enough." Aunt Gigi admitted that she and my dad had been together for years. My dad came clean and admitted that they started to get together once I got out of high school, and they'd been together ever since. I couldn't believe it. How did I not figure that out? I wasn't planning for it to be this way. But, since we were in the mood to drop bombshells, I introduced them both to my husband. My dad looked devastated and confused. "WHAT!", he shouted, the sound of his voice rippling through the house. Mike extended his hand and said, "it's good to see you again dad", emphasizing the D's in the word dad. My dad looked as hurt as I did when I saw him in bed with Aunt Gigi. After hauling the luggage to my room and showing Mike the layout of the house, I wanted to take him around Atlanta since it was his first time visiting.

After the shock of our family reunion Mike and I took off so I could show him my city, although still in disbelief. I drove him around to some of my favorite places like Piedmont Park, The Botanical Gardens and to see some friends. Angie moved back home with her parents after completing only two years of college and then she got her real estate license. I drove Mike to meet her and she loved him, but she called him soft. I wanted him to meet Joanna too, but she took a job as a high school guidance counselor working in Savannah. We enjoyed our trip to Atlanta and after a few days we were headed back to Philly. I was still trying to get over the shock of dad and Aunt Gigi that we didn't have sex the entire trip.

Shortly after we returned back to our little one-bedroom apartment in Philly, Mike was deployed to Iraq.

It wasn't long before I was hired as an administrator for the office of the director of finance with the city of Philadelphia. I fell in love with my work and quickly moved up through the various units. Mike was deployed most of our marriage. I missed him terribly, even though we didn't have much of a sex life he was like my best friend. I desperately wanted to start a family. I wanted a family so I wouldn't be so lonely when he was gone. My friends had all started having children and every time I opened my Facebook app somebody was having a gender reveal or sending baby registry announcements and I wanted my own baby announcement. Every time Mike came home I tried to get pregnant. I desperately wanted to be a mother. We tried to plan any short trips home around when I was ovulating, and I made him fuck me in every position. I was desperate to try almost anything because I hadn't had not one "pregnancy scare" with him.

After a few years in the cluttered apartment I decided to use the money left over from my trust to buy a house. After we closed on our house that we bought in Northeast Philly, I wanted Mike and I to christen every room in the house. The first night in the new house I laid naked and oiled at the top of the stairs and I told him that he had to fuck me doggystyle. I had been watching a lot of porn in his absence and I wanted to try new things and I knew that position could make him cum deep inside me. I watched a video online, on how to meditate to guide his sperm to my egg to increase the chance of fertilization. I was open to ideas to try different things to get me pregnant. Every time he came home from deployment I was naked and bent over when he walked in the front door. The sex never really got better. And it seemed like I would never get pregnant.

Throughout the years I continued to be the committed military wife I kept myself preoccupied with work. I worked my way up in City Hall, putting in a lot of time and I looked forward to when my husband would be home, to give me something else to focus on. Sometimes he was gone for six months and home for just three weeks before he had to leave again. We planned for him to complete ten years of service before his armed services separation. I was counting down the months until his retirement. I just wanted to be with him and have a real marriage and family with my husband laying beside me in bed, fucking me at night and us raising our children together.

When he was deployed we talked, and video chatted as much as we could together. Every once in a while he would indulge me with a little phone sex, but I knew he felt awkward and he wasn't comfortable doing it. Every year we tried to spend our anniversary together but this one year I knew he wouldn't be home to celebrate with me, but I was expecting his call, like he always did when he was gone on special occasions. On what would have been our sixth wedding anniversary I received the worst call a wife could ever receive. I answered the phone, initially questioning why it wasn't Mike's voice on the other end of the phone and learned my husband had been killed. He was traveling through Iraq when his unit was attacked. I dropped the phone, screaming in horror. I was hysterical as I laid in our bed looking over at his empty side of the bed. It was days before I could leave the house, my heart was in agony. Mike was more than my husband he was my friend, my companion. Our marriage wasn't perfect, but I knew that he loved me more than anything.

I mourned the death of my husband for a long time. Nothing prepares you for losing the one person you thought you would be with forever. Mike and I had a happy marriage. It wasn't exciting or sexually explosive, we loved each other. After Mike passed away it was a while before I tried to move on and date again, it was hard. I never thought I'd be a widow in my twenties.

CHAPTER FOURTEEN

I took a little time off to adjust to life without my husband. I traveled to Atlanta and spent some time at the home I grew up in. By this time, I'd come to terms with the idea of my dad and Aunt Gigi together. Out of curiosity I asked my dad about Victor. He seemed surprised that I asked about him and said that he was doing fine. He told me that Victor was in Europe on vacation with his wife and two kids. The sound of his name created a hard knot in my stomach. Victor was my first love. My first sexual experience. My first heartbreak. I was glad he wasn't in town while I was there. I was already an emotional wreck. I was glad that I didn't have to worry about going out and running into him. I spent a lot of time with Grandma Jean at her house. She cooked for me to comfort be and I tidied up the house for her. She was getting up in age and she didn't move around the same way anymore. I would drive to her house in the morning and she would cook us breakfast made of eggs, cream of wheat and scrapple. Our table conversations were usually centered around listening to the word of God. She made it clear that I shouldn't waste time if I wanted to start a family, because time was ticking, and I was almost thirty. I was grateful for my grandmother's wisdom even when I didn't want to hear it. My dad tried to convince me to stay in Atlanta, but I wanted to go back to my home and my job. After gaining ten pounds and feeling like I had the courage to move on, I ended my bereavement and went back to my empty home in Philly.

To lose the weight I'd gained by eating my grandma's food I joined a gym to drop the pounds and get in shape. I found a gym in Center City not too far from my job. I had been routinely going for a few months and seeing results as my clothes began to loosen. I decided to change my routine, thirty-minute jog on the treadmill and joined one of the fitness classes. I joined the cardio kickboxing class because it looked like fun. The class was full, so I found a spot in the back. The trainer was a hot, dark-chocolate, African guy wearing his gym shirt and jogging shorts that showed his enormous dick print. The class was an hour and since I'd been going to the gym for a few months I was able to keep up. After the class to my surprise the instructor walked over to me. I was putting my bag over my shoulder and grabbing my water bottle when he approached me.

"Hi, I'm Kendi. Thanks for joining my class today. You were really great", he added.

"Oh, thank you", I blushed. I didn't even know he was paying attention to me.

"What's your name?", he asked me.

"I'm Londyn", I extended my sweaty hand to him. He wiped his sweaty hand on his shorts and connected his hand with mine. His hands were big, and his grip was firm, but gentle.

"How did you like it?", he asked smiling at me.

I was blushing, turning shades of rouge and I was feeling nervous. "I enjoyed it. I think I'll come back again next week", I replied.

"Please do, come back next week and then come again and come again and come again", he said to me slowing down each time he said the word again, staring into my eyes." My pussy started to pulsate, and I felt like he knew it.

"I'm sorry", he excused, "I don't usually do this with participants in my class, he said charismatically, but there's something special about you and I want to get to know you and share your energy", he said to me. To my surprise with no makeup on and sweaty he asked me for my cell phone number. It had been almost a year since Mike passed and I was in no way ready to start dating, but I heard my grandma's voice reminding me that my biological clock was ticking and for me not to waste time sulking in self-pity. I needed to move on with my life, Mike wasn't coming back. I put my number in his phone and we continued to chat until it was time for his next class to begin.

He called me that night and he asked to come over. I was surprised by his eagerness but, I allowed him to come over. We stayed up and talked all night. He was really easy to talk to and he respected that I wasn't ready for sex yet. We began seeing each other regularly from the first day we met. I really liked him. We enjoyed going out together and sometimes he would come over and we would stay up talking and listening to music all night.

One night I invited him over for dinner after his last class. He was concerned about having to go home to take a shower because he didn't like taking showers at the gym. I told him he could just take a shower at my house.

Around seven that evening I heard a car door close and I met him at the front door. When I opened the door, I couldn't help but think to myself oh my fucking god this man is gorgeous. His skin was unblemished and youthful. His face was baby smooth, but he was my age. I opened the door to see him smiling at me holding his gym bag over his shoulder. I'd just put the food in the oven when he arrived. "Hi, Kendi" I said welcoming him in my home.

"Hey gorgeous" he greeted me with his full lips pressed to mine, using no hands.

I closed the door behind him admiring his fit body. "Let me show you to the guest room so you can take a shower," I said as we ascended the staircase.

"No, I want to take a shower in your room", he demanded.

"Oh," I said. "Sure, you can, but my guest room is nice too", I promised.

"I just want to be where I know your naked body has been because I think about it all the time."

"You do?", I sounded puzzled. "You think about me naked?" I asked for clarity. Kendi dropped his bag down beside my bed and pulled me to him swiftly and kissed me passionately. My body drifted towards his and he tightly wrapped me in his arms.

"I want you", he whispered to me grabbing my thick thighs. He glided me back on the bed and pulled my pants and panties off with ease. He lifted my shirt and began to suck my nipples while his thumb traced small circles around my clitoral jewel. He added his finger inside of my wetness, still switching between kissing me and sucking my breasts. His kisses began to descend to my stomach, then to my inner thighs. I felt my clit enter inside the warmth of his mouth and I gasped in pleasure. He sucked my pussy so hard, he had my hairy pussy dripping wet. He made my pink toes curl and I wanted to scream. He wouldn't stop. My legs locked around his neck, I was begging him to stop, even though I didn't really want him to stop. He ignored my pleas and continued pressing his tongue inside my pussy. I had cum so many times my clit felt numb. Finally, I couldn't take it anymore and I forced him off of me. He stood up and smiled down at me as I laid there with my legs shaking. Then he went into my bathroom and turned on the shower, stepped in two-sided glass shower and washed my pussy from his face and the sweat from his fit body. Once he had been in the shower for a few minutes, I climbed out of my queen-sized bed and joined him in the shower. I stepped in and pressed my wet body against his, kissing him. I leaned back in the shower and wet my face, before kissing him again. Then I crouched down and put his already hard dick in my mouth, slurping the spit in my mouth around his dick. He fucked the back of my throat until I gagged. Gagging made my mouth fill with spit and he forced me to my knees. I spit on his dick and stroked my slobbery wetness in my hand as the shower steamed up around us. I felt him tense up in my mouth, like he was about to cum and he lifted me to my feet and brought my lips back to his. He lifted my leg up and glided his hard dick deep inside me. After a few strokes I got caught up in the moment and allowed him to fuck me pressed against the steamy glass. Then I forced him to drop my leg once I remembered he didn't have on a condom. I quickly stepped out and I left him in the shower with a throbbing hard dick, while I threw on my robe and I went to go check on the food in the oven. After he took his shower he found me downstairs sipping on a glass of wine as I put the finishing touches on dinner. He told me he was starving, and he was ready to eat. He lifted me up and carried me to the table I had just set. I was taken aback at how easy he picked my big ass up. I leaned back on the cold counter top as he tasted my pussy like it was the first time, like the first time was just an appetizer. This time when he wanted to fuck he had a condom in his hand. He sat me on the edge of the counter, tossed my leg over his shoulder and fucked me until he came, and filled the condom. He came with a box of condoms and the box was empty when he left. My body needed it. We burned the food and ended up ordering pizza.

Things were going well between us. I continued to go to his cardio kickboxing class at the gym and we continued to see each other outside of class. Kendi slept at my house a few times a week and I began to look forward to being with him after my stressful days at the office. I was in the best shape I'd ever been in because I routinely joined his classes every Wednesday and he continued to work me out privately every night.

One week I had a meeting on Wednesday that I couldn't reschedule, so I changed things up and joined his Tuesday class. To my surprise when I got there another woman was kissing him good bye as though she just finished his class, and like he was her man. I walked up to Kendi and he looked very shocked and caught off guard. "Hey baby what are you doing here?", he asked in a low, nervous tone.

"I can't believe you, you lying motherfucker!", I yelled. I threw my capped water bottle at him and walked out of the workout studio. After that day I quit the gym and gained all the weight back. The next month I recognized my period was late. I panicked realizing the only man I had been with recently was Kendi. After giving myself an anxiety attack I took a pregnancy test and it was negative. Well, I took three pregnancy tests and they were all negative. The next morning, I woke up and had to pee as soon as I opened my eyes, like always. That's when I looked down and saw relief. Although I really wanted a child, I was so happy to see red on the tissue. Having a pregnancy scare is not as great as I thought it would be. I thanked God and promised to be more careful. Relieved and grateful I decided to chill on dating for a while.

CHAPTER FIFTEEN

I continued living in Philadelphia, dedicated to my work as the Director of Compliance for the City of Philadelphia and I kept myself too busy with work to have a real life. Dating began to annoy me, nobody could satisfy me, and I felt as though I was better off alone. I went back to school and got my master's degree from The University of Penn. By this time Grandma Jean had joined her daughter in heaven and it was just dad and Aunt Gigi at my graduation. I thought back to the night of my high school graduation. I remembered the smell of all the roses inside the Laurel Room at the Stanford Hotel, mixed with the scent of Victor's cologne. I got lost in the memory of feeling him enter me for the first time and then I began to feel lonely again when I realized I was daydreaming.

Some years passed before I dated again. It was just me and my little schitzu, Michelangelo. I got the little guy as a support dog, after Mike's death. One Saturday afternoon I was out enjoying my weekends off. I took Michelangelo out walking in Wissahickon Valley Park so he could run and play, and I could get some fresh air. There I ran into a guy I recognized from work.

"Hey, Ms. Ramsey", the familiar face spoke "how are you?" he asked with a smile. Michelangelo tugged on the leash to get my attention.

"Hi, I'm great. Alex right?" I asked hesitantly.

"Yeah, I'm flattered you know my name. I don't think we've ever directly spoken before" he stated with a smile.

I nodded to agree that we hadn't. "Please call me Londyn", I corrected. His smile was alluring, and he had my attention. He sat on the bench beside me and we continued to talk. I had no intention of spending the afternoon with him, but I did. We sat and talked for hours in the shade of the autumn foliage. I'd seen him many times around City Hall, but we never had any interactions before, we've just been in the same room together. Alex was the chief legal advisor for the city of Philadelphia and his office was on the fifth floor which was one floor above my office. Sometimes I would see him when we came through the metal detectors, sometimes we were in the same elevator together or even in a court room together, but we never spoke before now. He was very easy to talk to and really good looking. Michelangelo seemed to like him by the way he kept harassing Alex's hand with his tail.

"He likes you", I pointed out.

"Well I like him too" he patted Michelangelo on the head, "but I think I like his owner more" he added.

I looked at him blushing. "I've seen you so many times and I never knew what to say to you. I almost didn't come to the park today because I have so much work to do, but I'm glad I did", he smiled.

"How long have you worked at the hall?" I asked.

"About two years" he answered. "I remember the first time I saw you. It was at the employee basketball game against Delaware County. You were sitting in the bleachers alone and I wanted a reason to speak but I couldn't come up with anything, so I didn't. I'm a pretty private person and I didn't know how to step to you, without everyone in my business", he admitted. We continued to talk, sharing office stories and getting to know each other. Before it got too dark we exchanged phone numbers and agreed to talk soon. Before I could get home he'd already texted me.

Alex: It was nice to see you outside of CH. I hope we talk again real soon.

I replied back *I hope so too.*

The next day as I got dressed for work I put a little extra time and attention in my appearance hoping to see Alex. I didn't see him when I came in and I began to go about my day. About mid-morning as I sat at my desk analyzing a budget report, I heard a knock on the open door, and I looked up. It was Alex standing in the doorway to my office. He asked to take me to lunch and I accepted the invitation. He took me to a small Italian restaurant that had outdoor patio seating and we sat amidst the brisk breeze and we talked about work drama, ambitions and why we were both single. There were many lunch dates beyond that, and it felt strange because we would sneak away to the smallest and most random places so none of our colleagues would catch on to us.

We dated for about six wonderful months and things seemed to be getting serious with us. I was falling in love with him. He was spending most nights in my bed making love to me and I was considering giving him a key to my house. To keep things discreet, he would drive into Center City and I would use my free city pass and take SEPTA. I preferred not to drive and deal with traffic and public transportation allowed me to ride to work reading my favorite Ebony Payne-English poetry books.

We really enjoyed each other's company, we had so much in common. We were both from Philly, we were both passionate about giving back to the community and we loved the same corny romance comedies like, Fools Rush In and Boomerang. We talked a lot about our pasts, how it affected us as adults and what we wanted for the future, but we never talked about children. We'd talked about being married, but children were never part of the conversation. I could hear my grandma Jean's voice about my biological clock ticking away. One Friday night after a long and stressful week at work I invited him over to my house. When he arrived, I answered the door wearing nothing but a black apron, tied with a big bow draped against my bare oiled ass cheeks and pointed black stilettos. I made him hurry to shut the door, so my neighbors didn't see me. I walked him into the kitchen where I was almost finished cooking the lasagna. I was standing in front of the oven when he got down on his knees, spread my ass open and explored my crease with his tongue. "No, no, no" I moved his lips from mine and said, "That's dessert." "Damn girl you drive me crazy" he said looking like he wanted to take a bite out of me. I served dinner with wine and a little titty playing peek-a-boo from the side of my apron. He complimented me on my cooking and how sexy I looked. After dinner we walked over to the couch where I unbuttoned his suit pants and pulled his growing dick over the elastic from his boxer briefs. I began to stroke his hardness with my hand, spitting in my hand, making it slippery as I slowly stroked him. Then I leaned over and wrapped my tongue around his hardness. I got him nice and wet and then I sat on his lap and slid him inside of me. He grabbed my ass and bounced me like a carousel on his dick. His love making was intense and orgasmic, he would kiss all over my body, even my insecure parts like my stomach and my ass. We made our way up to my bedroom where he fucked me until I felt dehydrated. After the night of intense passion, I laid soaked in the wetness of our passion. "I love you", I whispered to him for the first time. He said the words back to me and it felt euphoric. "You keep putting it on me like that and I'm going to have to wife you up", he kissed me. "Oh yeah?", I blushed. This was my opportunity to bring up wanting to have a family, I thought. "The way you fuck me it's like you're trying to put a bun in the oven", I smirked. He didn't smirk. That's when he dropped a bombshell on me and told me that he didn't want to have any children. He was only three years older than me and he didn't have a child. How could he not want children, I thought? He tried to convince me that children are problematic, and we'd be better off with it being just the two of us. This was a game changer for me.

As much as Alex was an incredible guy and I was falling in love with him, I wasn't willing to compromise my dream of motherhood.

I immediately began avoiding him, I wasn't answering his calls and he wasn't spending the night and I wasn't inviting him over. He noticed my unusual behavior towards him and started calling me more frequently and I ignored every call. Finally, when I was ready to deal with the termination of our relationship I answered his call to invite him over one last time. I'd put all his personal items that he kept at my house in a rubber tote. I packed his clothes, his shoes, his tooth brush, his electric shaver and his small Bluetooth speaker. When he came to the door I was standing there and I handed him the tote full of his belongings and told him, "It's over". It was hard letting him go, because Alex was perfect for me, well almost perfect.

In the following days it was a little awkward seeing him around the building. I got jealous any time I saw him talking to another woman. I was relieved, when a few months later, I heard he was leaving to accept a position in D.C. with the United States Attorney General. I continued my position in the office of compliance and I continued to come home to Michelangelo, living my boring life.

CHAPTER SIXTEEN

Ten years passed me by since my husband died, and I still didn't have children or a man. I was beginning to come to terms that traditional motherhood may never happen for me and I was considering IVF or adoption.

One night as I was driving home from work through Center City, I got a call from Angie that she and husband number two were getting a divorce. She caught him cheating on her again. This time she caught him fucking his uber driver in their garage. I can't say I was surprised. He grabbed my ass on their wedding day when we were all on the dance floor doing the Cupid Shuffle, it made me sick to my stomach, but I kept quiet about it, because I didn't want to be the reason for her failed marriage. She invited me to her divorce party, that she planned to have in Cancun, Mexico for the upcoming weekend. It wasn't like me to take a trip at the spur of the moment, but I definitely needed a vacation. I hadn't spent more than a day with Joanna or Angie in years, I recalled. Although, this trip was unexpected, I was looking forward to hanging out with the girls and having some much needed fun.

I flew straight there and met them in Mexico. When we arrived at the resort that morning we saw that it was packed full of younger vacationers. None of us realized this trip was booked during college spring break. These spring breakers were loud and wild. Both, Angie and Joanna were mothers of teenagers and had been looking forward to being amongst the adults for a few days. We laughed it off and got settled in our individual rooms. We then met for mimosas at the hotel bar outside on the patio overlooking the water. I was sitting at the bar chatting with the girls when I saw a young man enter the bar area and grabbed my attention. He was tall with, brown skin and light eyes with thick curly eye lashes. His short dark hair was twisted in coils, his chest and legs were chiseled in the matching open shirt and shorts set he wore. He walked by me, making eye contact and just flashed his smile at me. He made me hot, my nose caught his trail of cologne. He smelled like a fine ass man. I cleared my throat and ignored it and resumed talking with the girls. We looked over the resort amenities and decided to go to the spa. We all needed to relax so we booked ninety-minute full body massages. I didn't realize how tense I was until I felt my body after the massage. Afterwards, Angie and Joanna followed up their massage with facials, but I wasn't interested in putting random products on my face. I told them I would meet up with them later and I left to do my own thing until we met up again later that night. My body still oiled up from my massage and wearing nothing but a white towel I entered the sauna to relax and detox.

It was dark in the hot, empty, wooden room. I sat down on the warm bench with my towel tucked tight against my breasts. My body was adjusting to the temperature in the room and I was beginning to sweat. Suddenly, my attention was directed to the door as I felt a burst of cool air once the door opened. That same young man that was checking me out earlier walked in wearing nothing but a towel around his waist. He looked to be about twenty years old. He walked in and then snatched his towel off, laid it on the bench and sat his naked exposed body on the towel.

I blushed trying not to look in his direction. But, I did steal a peek and damn he's fine, I thought.

He caught me looking at him and I got stuck in his stare. He broke the uncomfortable silence.

"Hi, I'm Nole Washington" he said to me smiling.

"Hi, I'm Londyn with a y," I said tightening my towel against my breasts, as if I didn't see his meat leaned against his leg.

"Londyn, that's one of my favorite places to visit. What brings you to Cancun Ms. Londyn?"

"I'm here on a girl's trip, celebrating my friends divorce" I added.

"Where are your friends?" he asked observing that it was just the two of us in the dark sauna.

"They're around here somewhere", I said tightening the loose towel around my breasts again.

Nole stood up so he could sit closer to me. He sat beside me, put my leg over his bare legs and I allowed his hand to caress my inner thigh.

We were beginning to vibe, when two older white women entered the hot sauna. They sat in the corner talking amongst themselves, talking very loud as if we weren't in there too. He continued to caress my inner thighs until his fingers met my moistness. He pulled his fingers from between my thighs and began to lick his fingers, smiling at me. The two older white women heard me moan before I could control my reaction and they hurried out of there mumbling as they exited.

We shared a laugh together, then things felt awkward again after the laughter ended.

"If I begged you would you take me to the best part of Londyn?" he asked still licking his fingers. I was turned on and offended. I couldn't believe this was happening. I hadn't been with many men since my husband died. This boy was almost half my age. But, I could handle a fling, it's not like I will ever see him again, I thought to myself. It was getting unbearably hot and I knew I would be getting out soon.

"It was nice to meet you Nole", I said as I was getting ready to make my exit.

He extended his hand to get my attention, "So, Ms. Londyn what are you doing this evening?" he asked.

The truth was I was probably just going to go back to my room and take a nap or go to the bar.

"I don't know yet" I replied. What will you do with the rest of the day?", I asked him.

"Me and some friends are going jet skiing later on today", he replied.

"Oh, that sounds like fun", I replied, "I have never been on a jet ski."

"Come with me" he begged.

"Oh no my big ass has no business on a jet ski", I responded laughing but serious.

"Oh, come on, and I've been on jet ski's plenty of times. I'm like a pro. Come on. Come with me" he begged. I lied and told him I already had plans. He still asked me to come with him. His begging was sexy.

I left him in the hot sauna so I could get up to my room to take a shower and enjoy the rest of my day. I thought of him as the hot water rinsed the lavender massage oil from my skin. Angie and Joanna were still at the spa, so I decided to change into my swimsuit and head down to lay out on the beach and soak in the sun. I chose to wear my leopard print two-piece swimsuit, that was high waisted to cover up my thick girl love handles. I put on my sunglasses and flipflops and headed downstairs. Once I got off the elevator I was greeted by the loud voices of wild youngsters. To my surprise Nole was down there with a group of his friends. I was reminded how young Nole was by his friend's interactions. He ran over to me, happy to see me.

"I wasn't expecting to see you", he said but he genuinely looked excited to see me. "Come hang out with me" he begged again. I was reminded that I had no plans and I agreed to join him. I felt out of place seeing them with his friends. I felt like I should have left before he saw me, but it was too late.

"Hey, Ms. Londyn with a 'y'!" he said greeting me with a hug. He turned to his friends and announced, "This is Londyn, she's gonna kick it with us." Everyone was cool and welcoming, and we walked together down to the beach to rent the jet skis. I was nervous mounting the water scooter and the water moved the jet ski from under me. I almost fell in the water and Nole was there to make sure I didn't lose my balance and he held onto me. Once seated I rode with my arms tightly wrapped around Nole as we ripped through the clear sea water. I felt amazing once we started riding out to the middle of the sea. I wasn't overthinking anything, I was allowing myself to live in the moment. We rode the jet ski out for a ways and then we just drifted for a bit enjoying each other's company. I was dying to know so I just abruptly asked. "How old are you?"

"I'm twenty-two" he replied.

"Damn," I said quietly.

"How old are you?" he asked me.

"You're not supposed to ask a woman her age", I reminded him.

"Well you asked me," he replied nonchalantly. He tried to guess "What are you thirty?" he asked.

"Oh, you are too kind. I'm almost forty" I replied.

He looked shocked that I was much older than I appeared, "Well, forty is the new twenty which means you just might be perfect for me," he said with a smile. I looked at him as if he couldn't be serious.

"I may be young but I'm not like these other young guys. I'm a man. I've had to be a man for a long time. I stepped up when my dad didn't", he added. "I'm about to graduate in a few weeks and I already have a job that I'll start after graduation. I'm not like these new cats' baby, I'm on my grown man shit. He said winking at me and then revved up the jet ski so we could head back to the shore. After returning the jet ski I left him on the beach with his friends. I went back to my room to meet up with my friends. They looked refreshed from their day at the spa. I looked tan from being out in the water with Nole. They grilled me about my tan lines, but I kept silent about my day with the college students.

We got dressed for dinner and headed down to the restaurant. Once downstairs one of Nole's friends recognized me from earlier and walked up to me. "Hey! What's up? We all just got down here too. Are you down for dinner?" he asked.

"Uh, yeah, sure" I replied. "If there is room for all of us. These are my friends Angie and Joanna" I pointed to my friends.

"Damn, your friends are sexy too," he casually inserted. "Come sit with us", he motioned for us to follow him. Joanna and Angie gave a look that told me they questioned how he knew me, but they cautiously followed along anyway.

The four of us walked over to the table with all the college spring breakers and joined them. Nole was surprised to see me and he walked over to me and greeted me with a warm hug and pulled out my chair.

Angie and Joanna remembered seeing him that morning and wondered what I had been up to all day while they were in the spa, enjoying their facials.

We enjoyed dinner and cocktails with them. Their young energy was nostalgic. Several times Angie and Joanna had to remember not to go into mom mode as they were talking about life experiences. After dinner we parted ways with the college crew and the three of us girls stayed up, drinking wine and reminiscing about being young and inexperienced until we passed out.

I saw him again, at breakfast the next morning. We were walking into the buffet area when I saw him. I pulled my sun glasses down to enjoy the clear view of that gorgeous young man. He walked past me holding his plate and he locked eyes with me and winked at me, then flashed his smile before turning the corner to join his friends who were seated outside.

"Girl that boy is fine!" Angie blurted.

I smacked her on the shoulder with my sunglasses and I silently agreed, "Yes, he is", as I stared at him like I wanted to eat him up.

That night we went to the hotel bar to sit and enjoy our last night in Mexico. I left Angie and Joanna at the bar after several shots of tequila, when I saw him enter the bar area. I stood up from the bar stool in my short, skin tight, pink floral, spaghetti strapped dress and sparkling flip flops. I walked up to him in front of all his friends, mine too and planted my lips on his. He didn't hesitate to kiss me back and he wrapped his arms around me. We could hear our friends talking about us, around us, but we didn't care. He pulled me onto the dance floor where I felt compelled to show him what an older woman could do to him. We danced to the rhythmic Latin beats, thriving off all the attention we were receiving from the room. I closed my eyes and got lost in the music dancing with him. I was enjoying the moment as he was grinding me from the back with his hands around my waist. After a few songs I reminded him that I'm older than him and I needed to sit down. We joined our friends at the bar who were laughing at me. "Can't keep up with the youngin', huh?" Joanna laughed. With the colorful strobe light illuminating our glasses we took more shots and then he stood up and pulled me back onto the dance floor. We stayed out on the dance floor so long, Joanna and Angie left and went upstairs to their rooms. I danced with him forgetting about reality and enjoyed every moment of him groping me and kissing my ear and desiring me. Sometime later that night, I told him my feet hurt and that I was tired. He offered to walk me to my room. He didn't hesitate at the opportunity to get me alone. We walked through the heavily air-conditioned lobby, into the elevator and up to my room. We stopped in front of my door and I looked him in his eyes to make sure he wanted to do this and there was no uncertainty in his eyes. We entered the room, his lips already locked to mine, our hands undressing one another. He was young and fine, and I could tell he had a big dick when we were dancing. But damn, I wasn't prepared for all that meat he was packing or that he could do what he did to my body. First he took me out to the balcony, leaned me over the rail, gently pulled my panties down and ate my pussy from the back under the moonlight. I couldn't believe he was so good to be so young. To enjoy tasting me from another angle he sat me in the chair on the small balcony and threw my legs over his shoulders, his face plunged between my thighs, slurping me up. With my pussy on his lips, he leaned up to kiss me. I leaned into him and he lifted me up, my legs wrapped around his waist, my juice in his mustache, he carried me to the bed. He laid me on my back his lips never parting from mine and he entered me. He could tell I liked it rough and he gave it to me just how I wanted it. I could feel the excitement in his rhythm, and he came quickly. He laid on top of me with his dick still inside me. I began to tighten my walls so he could feel me gripping him and he continued to stroke me until he came again. We fucked until the sun came out. I didn't know who came more times me or him. We eventually fell asleep naked in each other's arms to the sounds of birds chirping on the balcony. With the sunlight pouring into the room I woke up with a headache, vaguely remembering the night before. My eyes still blurry and unfocused I looked over and I saw Nole was still sleep, face down with his face pressed against the side of the pillow and naked in my bed. For a few seconds I wanted to believe I was dreaming. I was so hungover I couldn't remember if we used a condom. I knew I had to get him out of my room. I couldn't believe what I had done. I rubbed him on the shoulders to wake him and told him my friends were on their way and I couldn't let them see us like that, so he had to go. He gathered his clothes and got dressed. He asked me for my phone number so we could keep in touch, and I told him to just give me his. That's when my dream turned real. I met Nole in Mexico and he could be from anywhere in the world, so I allowed myself to enjoy a different part of me knowing after the trip I wouldn't have to see him again. He wrote down his cell phone number on the resort notepad on the nightstand. It's in that moment that things changed for me. "You have a four zero four area code, are you from Atlanta?", I questioned, trying to tame my hair with my hands looking concerned.

"Yes, born and raised. I'm a Grady baby", he said proudly. "Why do you ask?," he questioned.

"Because I grew up in Atlanta", I replied feeling uneasy.

"Oh, where do you live now?", he asked me.

All I could think is that I just fucked this boy and he doesn't know anything about me, and I don't know shit about him other than he laughs when he cums and he has a small birthmark that looks like a paw on his chest. "I live in Philadelphia, my dad still lives in Atlanta, so I visit a few times a year", I told him as I searched for my panties on the floor.

"I knew I wanted you when I first saw you. I honestly didn't think you were feeling me", he admitted to me. "But I knew I wanted my first time to be special and damn baby you are special. I was afraid I wasn't going to see you again but now you have another reason to come to the A. It must be meant to be", he said kissing my neck.

What the fuck, I thought! Did he say his first? My heart began racing and I felt like the room was spinning. I couldn't believe I took his virginity. I was trying to hurry him out of my room before he could ask me anything else. I couldn't get him gone fast enough. I gathered his clothes from the floor and handed him his clothes.

He still wasn't satisfied. "Call my number so I can save you in my phone," he requested. I reluctantly called him and hung up after two rings. Damn, now I couldn't just act like I lost his number. I told him he had to go and that I would call him later I pushed him out of the door just in time for my friends to see his exit. Moments after the door closed I heard knocks on my door.

Great, I thought! I knew they saw him leave my room.

"Girl! Girl! Did I just see that young tender leaving this room at seven o'clock in the morning?", Joanna scoffed.

"Did y'all hook up?", Angie questioned excitedly.

I shook my head before placing the pillow over my head confirming that we hooked up. "But it gets worse" I admitted. I had their attention. "I took his virginity" the room erupted in screaming.

"Girl shut up! I know you fuckin lyin'!" Angie exclaimed!

"Whaat??" Joanna sat on the bed in disbelief.

"Oh, it gets better" I said pacing in front of them. "He's from Atlanta and then I reiterated "and I took his virginity." The room abruptly went silent.

"Bihh!", Angie exclaimed.

"You didn't screen your one-night stand?", Joanna joked.

"Damn girl. Well at least you don't live in the A anymore, but that is a coincidence", Angie inserted.

"I know. I know", I said shaking my head. "Our flights leave tonight", I announced. "Let's pack up and figure out how to leave Mexican skeletons in Mexico."

I felt like I was doing the walk of shame as I was checking out of the resort. I managed to get to the airport without Nole texting me or calling me. But, when I got off the plane I saw I had several messages from Nole and Aunt Gigi. I needed time to think about my response to Nole. Time went from a few minutes to a few hours and I still hadn't returned one message or one phone call. I didn't know how to respond so I didn't. Eventually that night he stopped calling and texting me. I felt bad but I had already gone too far. He was too young for me, and I knew that feeling and I didn't want to lead him on any further. I wanted to let our fling remain in Mexico. I planned to resume my boring, routine life in Philly and forget about Nole.

CHAPTER SEVENTEEN

My life changed the next morning. In the midst of
me avoiding Nole's calls I failed to call my aunt Gigi
back. She called me and woke me up super early the
next morning. When I answered the phone, she
sounded relieved, and immediately began yelling at
me for not calling her back. She was calling to tell
me that my dad was not well. She told me that he'd
had a heart attack and he was in the hospital. He was
in critical condition and I needed to get there right
away. I apologized for not being there and told her I
would be there soon. I immediately began to search
for flights. I couldn't get a flight out that night, so I
booked a flight to Atlanta for the next morning. The
morning of my flight I called my dad and told him I
loved him and that I was coming to see him. He told
me not to worry about him, but Aunt Gigi told me to
hurry. And I felt the urgency in her voice. I'd only
heard her once life that in my life once before. I
called my boss on the way to the airport and he told
me to take as much time off as I needed, and I
rushed to see about my dad. I was nervous about
going home. Of all the trips I've ever taken home
over the years this one felt different. I thought about
what if I saw Victor? What if I saw Nole? I couldn't
focus on that I was racing to get to my father, I

reminded myself. My aunt Gigi called me when I landed and told me to hurry. I rushed off the plane and jumped in an Uber. The airport was crowded from spring break travelers and it took me forever to get out of Hartsfield-Jackson. Once I arrived at the hospital I received a text from Aunt Gigi that said, *he just passed.* I screamed in shock, reading the message repeatedly. I was in disbelief that I got there just minutes too late.

I went straight to the hospital room where Aunt Gigi was still sitting at his bedside. I held my dad's warm hand and whispered to him how much I love him and to kiss mommy for me. I was so angry at myself for not being there sooner. Had I been my normal boring self I would have been at home when I heard of my dad's heart attack instead of traveling back from some young out of the country dick.

My Aunt Gigi and I made his final arrangements together. The outpouring of love and support I received due to my father left me deeply moved. I was overwhelmed by the love and support received by so many people that my father impacted. He was a good man and a generous figure in the community. We planned his homegoing to celebrate him the way he would have wanted. The morning of my father's funeral I woke up in my childhood bed after a sleepless night. That night for the first time in many years I dreamed that I was with both my mom and my dad. My eyes popped open at the sound of my alarm, realizing my parents were finally together again and I was here alone without them. I was having a hard time processing it all and I wondered how my aunt Gigi was feeling.

I couldn't believe it was the day I had to bury my dad. Not my dad, I thought. I got dressed in an all-black dress that I never wanted to wear again and rode in the limo with Aunt Gigi to the church. It was a big church and hundreds of people were in attendance. Once we arrived in front of the massive church I began looking around for familiar faces, but I couldn't focus on anything because the reality of where I was and what I had to do sank in. Once inside I walked down the somber aisle with Aunt Gigi on my arm, clenching her hands, as we approached my father's lifeless body in the casket. Seeing him like that and knowing that would be the last image of him in my memory I almost lost it, as tears began to pour down my bronzed cheeks. I forced myself to find the strength to get through that moment of viewing his body, feeling everyone's eyes on my back. I also needed to be strong for my aunt who described my dad as the love of her life. Her hands were trembling in mine as we stood there together admiring how he still looked strong and powerful. Although they never got married I knew my dad loved her. I just couldn't believe he was gone. I stood there observing what looked different and what looked the same about him and feeling like I wanted to climb in the casket with him. For a moment I allowed myself to imagine him getting up and this all being a dream. Then the organ began to play and brought me back to reality. We took our seats so they could close the casket and drape the red roses along the top.

The service honoring my father was beautiful, the choir sang *Take me to the King*, my dad's favorite gospel song and there were so many tributes to him. We played a short video of him from different moments throughout his life, with included old home movies that included my mom and my Grandma Jean. The memorial video had everyone in tears, my aunt Gigi lost it seeing my mom and dad together. I'm sure many in attendance never put two and two together that she was with her dead sister's widower. Following the video, the pastor delivered a sermon high-lighting my dad's remarkable journey in life and how he allowed God to work through him to build and educate the black community on financial success. After his sermon the pastor then granted a few individuals a two-minute opportunity to share their thoughts. I was sitting on the front pew, next to Aunt Gigi when I saw him. At my father's funeral I saw Victor for the first time in twenty years.

He walked up to the wooden podium resting his hands on the side, as he looked over the flowers strung over my father's now closed casket. He began to speak very powerfully as, if public speaking were second nature to him. I no longer questioned if I would recognize his voice. I closed my eyes and recited things he once said to me. I wasn't sure if he saw me in the crowd. Would he even recognize me,

I thought? Towards the conclusion of his brief address, he directed his gaze in my direction as he uttered, "...and he bestowed upon me the most precious gift one could ever receive."

He stepped down off the stage, walked by me and took his seat behind us.

After the service was over many people walked over to me to offer their condolences, before heading into the hall to feast on their catered meal. I didn't have much of an appetite and I was getting ready to leave the church when he walked over to me.

"Londyn Banks", he said surprised to be standing there with me. "Wow, it's good to see you. It's unfortunate that it's under these circumstances, my condolences", he added.

"Yes, I know this is so unexpected. Thank you for your kind words", still in shock that I was standing there talking to Victor and at my father's funeral.

"We're all so overwhelmed with grief over your father's passing. I learned a lot from your father in my career. I owe everything to him," he shared.

"Wow, Victor, I can't believe I'm seeing you after all this time" I paused taking him all in. After all these years he had not aged much. He was still fit, charming and attractive. "Thank you again for those kind words. I can't believe I haven't seen you, in what... in twenty years", I questioned thinking about all the time that had passed.

"How long are you in town?," he asked.

"I'm not sure" I replied, surprised that he inquired.

"I know you are going through a lot during this difficult time, but I would love to take you out to dinner tonight and catch up", he said to me.

I paused for a moment before I answered. "I'm flattered Victor" I paused again, I knew it shouldn't matter but I asked anyway "and what about your wife?" I questioned intensely staring at him until he answered me.

"We have a lot to catch up on. I've been divorced for many years" he clarified.

"Oh", I said trying not to show my enthusiasm. I admitted that I wasn't sure how long I would be in town. "I'm here just long enough to handle my father's affairs", I confirmed. "I still live in Philadelphia, but I'm free tonight." I agreed to meet him for dinner that night and we finally exchanged phone numbers.

That night as the sun began to set he picked me up from the house. My Aunt Gigi was in my bedroom, sitting with me on my bed talking to me about how much she missed my dad when the doorbell rang. I forgot to tell her I was leaving. She questioned who could be at the door. I jumped up off my bed and hurried down the steps to greet Victor at the door. I was too slow to the door to get out the front door before she saw who was there. My aunt Gigi made her way behind me, her bright colored Moomoo dress flowing through the foyer. She was curious to see who it was at the door. I'm too grown to be this nervous, I thought. I dreamed about what awaited me on the other side of the door. I opened the door and Victor was standing there holding a single red rose up to his face. He handed me the rose, then wrapped his arms around me. "My, my girl you are still beautiful and thick in all the right places", he said admiring my body. Unsure of how to respond, I just looked at him with my matured eyes and cleared my throat to get his attention. He pulled back from my body when he saw we were not alone. "I should have known there was something between you two back then," Aunt Gigi blurted, with her arms across her large breasts. "My Spidey senses were going off, she continued. "It's good to see you again too Gigi. I'm sorry for your loss," he said solemnly. "Thank you Victor. Elton was my everything and I can't believe I have to live without him." She began to cry, and I directed her to the guest room where she'd been sleeping the past few nights. She wasn't able to sleep in their bed. She said she just wasn't ready for that yet.

"It's not like that Aunt Gigi", I lied.

She turned around and I heard her muffle "It better not be". Once Aunt Gigi was on her way back upstairs, Victor walked me out to the car, he opened my door and we drove off to the restaurant.

I was nervous being around him. This almost forty-year-old woman was sitting next to him feeling like a naïve teenage girl again. It wasn't until he squeezed my thigh that it triggered that unwavering sexual desire for him, and I sat back in my seat. He sensed the tension and he began to tell me how great it was to see me after all these years. Hearing these words from him had me feeling less anxious. I remembered when we were a thing and how he made me feel wanted and desired. We began to catch up in the car, riding to the restaurant. He quickly filled me in on current events. I learned that he still worked for my father's company as the chief of operations and was acting CEO after my dad's passing. Oh, and I learned that he was single. He admitted that he and his ex-wife Lisa had attempted to reconcile not long ago, but he soon realized he didn't want to get back together with her. Hearing that he was single sparked my curiosity and I felt flushed. I told him I too was single, and my life was simple and uncomplicated. "I just work, work, work," I laughed. He spoke great things about my dad and their experiences over the years. Just hearing him mention my father gave me chills. It had only been a few days and I was still in shock over his death. We arrived at The Steak House and pulled up to the valet. The Atlanta air welcomed me as Victor opened my door and then walked me inside the elegantly lit restaurant.

The restaurant was filled with small round tables dressed in white linen, shined silverware and wine glasses made of crystal. "Reservation for Crawford", he assertively told the hostess. I was still in awe that I was on a real date and not a secret rendezvous with Victor Crawford.

CHAPTER EIGHTEEN

I had butterflies in my stomach as he pulled my chair out for me and we sat down at the table. When we were together before we could never go out as a couple and risk being seen together. We were always trying to avoid my family or his wife seeing us or finding out about us. We'd always find clever places to meet or sneak off to, but always careful that we weren't seen together by the wrong people. Once seated across from him it took a while for me to stop fidgeting. My foot was shaking like a rattlesnake in my heels under the table. It became noticeable when the crystal on the table began to shake. He placed his hand over mine to comfort me and I began to relax a little bit. But, I wondered if he remembered me, the way I remembered him. Suddenly, his attention was directed to something that I wasn't sure if he would notice.

"Wow! You still have it after all this time", he said observing me wearing the pandora charm bracelet that he gave me years ago. I found it in my old jewelry box in my room at my dad's house and decided to wear it for this occasion and didn't take it off afterwards. Over wine and a three-course dinner, we reminisced and shared all the feelings that remained suppressed all these years. Ever since I saw him at my father's funeral memories of us together invaded my mind. I remembered the night of my high school graduation when I lost my virginity to him. It was like I felt myself in that moment laying in the bed in room 526 of the Stanford Hotel. I closed my eyes remembering how he laid me on the bed and slid my panties over my feet with his mouth. He slowly kissed from my pierced navel down to my lips. When I felt his tongue enter my body I jolted, sitting up in my seat, my eyes wide open, realizing I had been daydreaming. He asked me was I ok. I had to remind myself I was with him, I didn't have to day dream any more. I told him how special it was for me that he was both my prom date and my first. "Oh yeah" he smirked with his white teeth peering through his smile. "I wasn't so sure it would happen", he confessed. "I didn't want to hurt you, but damn girl there was something about you. I just couldn't resist you. It would have been detrimental to me if your father or Lisa ever found out about us", he chuckled.

"Yeah, I thought we were caught a couple of times." I admitted to him how envious I was over his wife. "I know she sensed my feelings for you. I remember thinking about you getting a divorce so we could be together. I was young and dumb", I laughed sipping my glass of White Zinfandel. He told me about his messy divorce, and his estranged relationship with his son who was twenty-two years old and in college and his daughter who was twenty living at home with her mother. He hadn't spoken to his children in years. His son stopped speaking to him after the divorce and changed his last name to his mother's maiden name. I could tell from the change in his tone that the details regarding the relationship with his children was hard for him to talk about. I changed the direction of the conversation and I shared with him that I got married right out of college but that my husband died in the military, that we never had any children and I never remarried. "I married my work", I laughed with my laugh slowly fading at that reality. Technically this was the first date I'd had in a while. Was this a date, I questioned to myself? I still couldn't believe I was out to dinner with Victor Crawford. Victor was now fifty years old, with a salt and pepper beard heavily salted but, still fine and charming. He was even more experienced and articulate; the deep sound of his voice was still sexy and brought back so many memories from my senior year in high school. I felt like a young girl again. He was bringing me peace and was a welcomed distraction at a time when I was emotional and grieving.

After dinner was over I didn't want the night to end. While waiting for the valet he put his arms around me and brought my lips to his. His kiss was memorable. I felt a familiar electricity travel through my veins, igniting a spark between my thighs. I asked him if he remembered where he would meet me when we would sneak around. He looked at me and smirked. He turned and told the guy at the valet to hurry up. Instead of just telling me, he drove me to the dark vacant parking lot of what was once Taylor's department store. Taylor's went out of business a few years ago and the building became a small business resource center. He put the car in park, unsnapped my seatbelt and brought his lips to mine. I was flooded with young eighteen-year-old girl emotions. I felt a tidal wave of emotions flush over me. I felt vulnerable and I wanted to live out what I couldn't twenty years ago. I whispered to him "I want you so bad. I want you to make love to me." He told me to put my seatbelt on and he drove off. I didn't know where he was taking me, but I was excited along the ride. I rubbed the inner crease of his thighs and watched him squirm as his pants began to swell. We pulled up to a big beautiful, two-story brick house in a gated community. Over dinner I'd learned he got the house, she got alimony in the divorce settlement and realized it was the same house he owned when he was married. I had envisioned being in this house so many times, I thought to myself as I stepped inside. I began looking around at all the dark elaborate furniture. There were large flat screen televisions on the walls in each room lined with black leather sofas and mahogany decor. My eyes roamed the area for something to grab my attention like family photos or a women's earring left on the counter. I didn't see any of that, he'd turned the place into a modern bachelor pad equipped with a screened in hot tub. I'd learned over dinner that he dated women but never anything serious. He disturbed the silence of my thoughts when he turned on the music from his iPhone and the sounds of R&B artist Gerald Levert began to play from the Bluetooth speakers hidden in the corners throughout the house. I was a little tipsy from all the wine at dinner, I continued to walk around slowly taking in the fact that I was with Victor in his house, we were both single, grown and still attracted to one another. He took my hand and guided me through his home and up the stairs. I followed behind him upstairs to his bedroom, where he made love to me, like it was the first time. He kissed my shoulders and sucked the perfume from my neck, exploring my breasts with his hands. I pulled my arms through the sleeves and stepped out of my dress. Victor grabbed me, wrapping his arms around my ample ass before taking my breasts into his mouth as I stood with my toes in the soft carpet. Then he sat me back on his king size bed and removed my black lace panties and dropped them on the floor. I was so glad that I shaved before I left Philly. I arched my back over the bed, and inhaled as his lips explored my inner thighs, my body melted into his mouth. I put my mind on autopilot to allow myself to enjoy every moment of this experience. He took off his clothes while admiring my body until he chiseled brown skin was bare and his body became familiar to me again. I remembered how when his dick was hard it curves to the left. He leaned over me, grabbed my left thigh, kissing my lips, he entered me, saying my name as he stroked deep into my wetness. The sound of my name from his lips was turning me on and making me creamier. Sex with Victor was better than I remembered. He made me climax harder than I had ever come with him before. As I laid naked beneath his passion-soaked body, I wondered, if I was crazy for doing this, but I couldn't get enough of him. One orgasm after the next, my feelings for him resurfaced and I felt like I was eighteen all over again, except I was thirty-eight and this time it felt different because this time the thought that we could be together was real.

CHAPTER NINETEEN

In the days following the funeral Victor was so comforting and compassionate. We'd seen each other every day and every night since the day of the funeral. I was unsure about how people would react to us being together. Everyone in the company was familiar with us both, just not us together, but we didn't care, and I was prepared to handle the comments or whatever came next. Enjoying the freedom of being together Victor and I quickly became quite comfortable and very bold, as we were not shy about being seen together. I planned to go back home to Philly soon and I was trying to figure out how I could manage a long-distance relationship with Victor.

Before I left to go back home to Philly my father's attorney Garrett Stark gathered myself, Victor and all the board members together to discuss the details of the current business operating agreement and to make a big announcement. That morning, after waking up in his arms, Victor drove us to the corporate office in Midtown to attend the board meeting, he was anxious about the announcement. He was so upbeat and in a great mood as we pulled into his executive parking space. I hadn't been there in years, the building looked bigger than I remembered. It was a brick, three-story building near West Peachtree Street filled with many offices. I remember the feeling I had walking into my dad's office for the first time since he died. When I opened the door to his office I almost expected him to be in his chair, looking up at me with his pen in his hand, on the phone. The fact that I was looking at his empty chair but in my mind I saw him sitting there in his suit and designer watch gave me chills. Knowing that I knew he would never be in that chair again seemed surreal. I walked over to his desk and sat in his hard leather chair and looked around at his desk. He left his desk as if he expected to come back to it. His desk was disheveled, but his desk drawers were locked. There was a family photo poised on his desk of my mom, my dad and me. The photo of us was taken when I was eight, one summer at Dorney Park in New Jersey. I remember that summer I was finally tall enough to ride one of the big rollercoasters. We looked so happy, everyone in denim shorts and matching t-shirts, smiling in the blazing sun. I remember how incredibly hot it was that year and how much my dad complained about spending four dollars on bottled water. That was our last trip together as a family. With tears welled in my eyes I continued to glance over his desk. He had a desk calendar with notes and appointments written on it. I noticed he had my birthday circled which was coming up soon and another date, to which I didn't know the significance. Then my eyes began roaming around the room, admiring his many awards and achievements.

I knew it had grown, but I guess I didn't realize how big the company had become. My dad started the company thirty years ago after he worked for an awful company in Philadelphia that he said didn't value him or pay him enough for his time or worth. He said that was going to be his last job where he could be treated like another nigga, so he quit. That's when he took the money he inherited from my mother, moved us to Atlanta and started his own investment company, E.J. Banks Capital Inc. When he moved us down here when I was a little girl, I remember he told me he wanted to be the most successful black man in Atlanta. He wanted to create more knowledge and access to investing and commercial lending opportunities for the black community. The company had grown over the years to become a powerhouse and has landed on the cover of Forbes magazine. Those were among his many Black Enterprise magazine covers framed on each wall. He worked hard and ultimately made the decisions he felt were needed to make sure his vision was carried through. He worked his entire adult life to build his business into the empire it's become, grossing millions each year. I was so proud of my dad for all that he achieved. Suddenly, my attention was redirected when I heard someone walk in. Victor came to the door and asked what I was doing in there.

"Nothing", I replied getting out of the chair, then I turned the light off and shut the door to my dad's office.

I walked into the boardroom behind Victor, to what we expected to be the formal announcement of Victor Crawford as CEO. Victor had been my dad's right-hand man and remained dedicated to my dad for twenty years. It had been discussed, when he got the position as chief of operations that one day my dad would leave the company to Victor, since he thought of him like a trusted friend. Victor brought in more revenue than anyone else in the company, except my dad, and he was loyal. My father's attorney Garrett stood up and we all braced ourselves for what we expected to be my father leaving Victor in control of the company, but to everyone's surprise, Garrett was reading a notarized document stating that my father left me controlling shares and named me as successor to run his company as the new CEO.

This took Victor, the board members and especially me completely by surprise. This bombshell left me speechless. Victor looked at me with disdain in his eyes and I didn't know what to say. I was certain that everyone in that room, including myself, believed Victor was going to be announced as the new CEO. I wasn't sure if I accepted the role. This was a huge decision and I hadn't even thought about moving back to Atlanta. I stood up in front of everyone in the room. "Wow", I said pausing as I gathered my thoughts. "My dad was always full of surprises", the room erupted in laughter. "I just want to say I'm humbled and honored that my dad would name me to run his amazing company. This is very much unexpected, he never shared this with me" and I took a deep breath. "This is a lot to think about, as you all know I don't even live here", I laughed. The room shared in my laughter. "I will do my best to make my father proud." I folded my hands in front of me and looked over at Victor who looked away. Everyone in the room then stood up in applause. Victor was the last one in the room to stand. I noticed him reluctantly clapping. All eyes were on me so, I maintained my demeanor and I hoped this wouldn't put any strain on our emerging relationship.

Once the meeting was adjourned I observed Victor attempting to rush out of the boardroom without speaking to me. I excused myself from the room and caught up with him near the elevator. "Victor wait!", I shouted, as I quickly walked over to Victor who clearly was trying to avoid me. "Victor I'm as shocked about this as you are, but please let's not let this come between us. Let's figure this out together." I said to him kissing him on the lips. Victor leaned into my kiss and assured me that he would continue his role as chief of operations and that he would support me with anything that I needed. "I have your back my love", he said embracing me. Garrett told me that he needed to speak with me, but Victor insisted that we had to go, and I told Garrett I would contact him later on.

That night we went back to his house and he suggested that we get in the hot tub and relax. I stripped and allowed the jets to hit my naked body like I was getting a Swedish massage. Victor then sat down and grabbed me placing me on his lap. That night I let him take all of his frustration out on my pussy. He fucked me so deep it hurt. I was about to tell him to stop when he whispered, "I never fucked a CEO before". Him saying that made me feel like he might be ok with this and I didn't make him stop. After he made me cum until I was tired and my pussy was throbbing we went upstairs and we laid naked in bed, with his arms holding me close to him. He reassured me that if it became too much I could always step down and he would take over. He said it so comforting and supportive. I thanked him for being so available to me and I told him I wanted to work together as partners. The truth is I never wanted this position and I hadn't thought about it before now. But what I knew was my mother made sure that when the opportunity presented itself I would be ready and equipped with the education and intellectual capacity to be successful at anything and after some thought I knew that if this is what my dad wanted then there had to be a reason and I wanted to honor him, and I was not about to let my parents down.

Over the next few weeks I flew back and forth to Philly as I prepared to remain permanently in Atlanta. I resigned from my position at City Hall. I donated my home to my alma mater, to offer housing to students from low income households and we named the housing space Jeanette Banks House after my mom. Then me and Michelangelo moved back into my childhood house with my aunt Gigi, until I figured out where I was going to live in Atlanta.

During my last trip back to Atlanta, while rushing through Hartsfield Jackson airport, I was on my phone scrolling through messages and I accidently answered a call from Nole. Fuck! I said to myself before bringing the phone to my ear. "Hey Nole, what's up?" I asked very short, annoyed with myself for answering.

"Hey, I've been worried about you. You haven't returned any of my calls", he said with sounding happy to hear my voice on the phone.

"I'm sorry Nole I have a lot going on right now." He pleaded with me to meet him somewhere to talk, because he wanted to see me.

I explained to him that my father had just died, and it was not a good time and that he had to stop calling me. He was genuinely sorrowful when he offered his condolences. Then I felt bad. I remembered what it felt like to be young and in love with someone older and unavailable, with all your feelings wrapped in knots. I can't even believe I put myself in this situation, I thought to myself. I needed to give him closure the right way so he could move on from me. I agreed to meet him to talk soon.

CHAPTER TWENTY

I began to spend my days in the office and my nights in Victor's bed. I was still trying to feel things out with him while I was adapting to my changing life. Things began so perfect with us after all these years but now this shake up naming me as the CEO has shifted our relationship. Sometimes he seemed supportive by explaining and giving me back stories on clients and prospects and sometimes he showed me a side of him that alarmed me. I was eager to learn about every aspect of the business, but I felt like he shared just enough of what he wanted me to know and often avoided answering me when I questioned certain business activity. At times, I felt like he didn't have time for me unless we were fucking.

I was sitting at my desk, feeling lost in my emotions when my phone notification got my attention. It was a text from Nole.

Hey beautiful. I'm just thinking about you. I can't get you off my mind. I want to see you.

Feeling emotional and lonely I responded to Nole and agreed to meet him, and I replied *OK,* and I continued to text him the details about us meeting up.

Later that day, I was getting ready for dinner with Nole when Victor walked into the bedroom where I was spraying myself with perfume. The sweet mist filled the air as he approached me.

"Where are you going?", he questioned sternly.

"I'm going to dinner with Angie" I lied. "Do you want to come with me?", I asked confidently knowing that he would not accept the invitation.

"Have fun", he said. He kissed me on the forehead, "I'll probably be home late", he announced as he exited the room.

That evening I met with Nole at one of my favorite seafood restaurants in Atlanta. He pulled out my chair and placed my napkin in my lap. He was a gentleman to me, and I felt terrible that what I had to tell him was going to crush him. Over dinner I explained everything that had happened since we left Mexico. I told him that I was seeing someone and that I couldn't see him anymore. "Londyn, you make me feel alive in ways I've never felt before. I've fallen in love with you. Let me be the man who gives you everything you deserve", he pleaded.

I was so tempted by his sexiness and his irresistible charm. He tempted me the way Victor once tempted me as a young girl. I looked into Nole's eyes and it was like looking at Victor, which was eerie to me. There were things about him that reminded me of Victor like his eyes and his voice. The wine in my glass began to get low, the chatter around us faded and the table fell silent until Nole broke the uncomfortable silence by asking me a question I wasn't prepared to answer. His eyes became fixated on a bruise he saw around my wrist. I hadn't thought to wear longer sleeves to hide it. The day before, as I was getting ready for a board meeting, Victor and I got into an argument about auditing the bank accounts, because I noticed many of the accounts used the same mailing address and I asked him what he knew about that. Victor squeezed my pandora bracelet into my wrist so tight it left a bruised imprint from each charm in my skin and then he told me those were his accounts and I didn't need to question him about his clients. I smiled at Nole trying to play it off by acting surprised as if I didn't notice it.

Nole saw through my faux smile, "Does he hurt you Londyn?" he asked with concern, taking my hand into his.

"No!", I shouted abruptly, snatching my hand away. "He's never hit me", I quickly added. But, he has pushed me around and sometimes the switch on his temper scares me, I thought to myself, but I didn't say that aloud.

"Londyn I know we've only been in each other's lives for a short time, and I'm a little younger than you", he tried to add as if a seventeen-year age difference wasn't a big deal, "but I love you and I want to be with you. I didn't have the best example of how to be a man, but I know what I don't want to be. My father is a terrible man. He was abusive to my mother and he cheated on her. I saw how my father hurt my mother and I knew I never wanted to be like that man. That's why, when they divorced I took my mother's last name. Whoever this guy is he doesn't know how precious you are. I know you think I'm crazy because we just met but, I know I can make you happy if you let me," he begged.

 I took a sip of the sweet red wine, "Nole you are sweet and kind and and fine as fuck and you will make some young woman very happy. For a virgin you sure knew how to put it on me," I giggled and then I got back serious. "But, I just can't get past the age difference and I just need you to respect that. We can be friends, but nothing more," I added. He reluctantly agreed to contain his feelings for me so that we could still be friends and after dinner we went our separate ways. I knew that would be my last time out with Nole. I was trying to forget about Nole and his young thick dick and focus. I needed to direct my attention towards my emerging life and understanding my role as a CEO.

CHAPTER TWENTY ONE

I was on a mission to prove that I would be as successful as my father or better. As I spent more time at the office, it became more evident that Victor felt that he should have taken my father's place controlling the company. His sarcasm about not being in charge when anything happened was becoming too much to tolerate. I was getting sick of his slick, disrespectful comments about me running the company or running the company into the ground, but I didn't say anything. I questioned myself if he made the comments because I'm a woman or because he just thought he was better than me. I still loved Victor, but I wasn't certain about the future of our relationship.

Tension was thick between Victor and I in the office. I could tell it made the employees uncomfortable, I noticed how they would avoid being in the room if Victor and I were together. I've known many of the individuals employed by the company for nearly my entire life. It felt bizarre to me that they were working for me. I wanted to earn their respect as a leader, but I had some big shoes to fill. I spent every day in the office trying to learn the business. Somedays Victor was more willing to help than others, but he didn't like me asking a lot of questions.

I moved into my dad's office, adding my own décor without removing his. The desk was still locked, and apparently nobody had a key to his desk. My office was across the hallway from Victor's smaller office. I asked Victor if he had a key to the desk, but he told me that he did not. I asked him to come in and see if he could open it. He tried to pry it open, but he wasn't able to get it unlocked. He looked down at the desk and saw the date my dad circled.

"Londyn you have a birthday coming up?" he asked.

"Yes, in just a few days. My dad always did something special for me. It going to be hard to spend my first birthday without him here," I admitted.

"There's nothing going on around here. You should take the rest of the day off. Go check on Gigi. She's still a wreck," he said concerned.

I smiled, happy that we seemed to be in a good place, "You're right it's been a few days since I checked on her." I finished up my work that day and I drove over to see my aunt who was still grief stricken.

I was always so happy to be with my aunt. But when I walked in the house my mood changed from comfort to concern. She looked as though she had not been taking care of herself. I looked around, the house was a mess and that was not like her to be in a messy house. I called Victor once I got there to let him know about her and that I may stay at little later to remain with her and straighten up, but he didn't answer my call. While chatting with my aunt I made her something to eat. Nothing fancy just some quick shrimp alfredo. Meanwhile as she was enjoying the food I began to straighten up the downstairs a bit. I sent Victor a text, but he didn't respond to that either. Feeling a little tired I sat at the kitchen table for a while, talking to my aunt about life's unknown plans, while checking my phone every few minutes. I had been at the house for some time and it was bothering me that he hadn't responded to me. I knew that even if he was extremely busy he would have checked his phone at least once or twice by now. After several hours of no response from Victor, I told my aunt that I needed to go. I was worried that something may have happened to him. She didn't want me to go, she begged me to slow things down with him. "But what if he was in an accident and he needs me!" I gently shouted. I grabbed my purse, then kissed my aunt's cheek and hopped in my car and took off. I wasn't sure where I should go. I called Victor's phone with no answer on repeat. First I went by the office, but he wasn't there, nobody was. Then I sped off towards his house. When I pulled into the driveway I immediately noticed his car wasn't there, but before I got out of the car he finally called me back.

"Victor where are you?" I demanded as soon as I answered the phone.

"I'm on my way home" he said nonchalantly ignoring the panic in my voice. "I have a surprise for you" he continued.

"Victor, I was so worried about you. It's not like you to ignore my calls like that. I thought something happened to you", I said relieved, on the verge of tears. He reiterated that he was planning something for me and that's why he had to be MIA for a few hours. I was less angry as my heartrate began to return to normal.

He pulled up to my car and waved his phone in my face to show me what he had been up to. To my surprise for my thirty-ninth birthday Victor took me on a private jet to Bimini, a small island a short distance from The Bahamas, just the two of us, relaxing on the beach, making love from sun up to sun down. We had a small hut on the water with a hot tub inside, I was wet most of the trip. The trip was perfect it was the old Victor that I once knew. The sex was amazing, despite how he may have come off sometimes, I knew he loved me. It wasn't until we were finished packing up so we could head to the airport that the other Victor resurfaced after I took a call from my father's attorney Garrett. I had been in more frequent contact with Garrett since my dad passed, but I was still uncertain why he was calling. He asked to meet with me to discuss something he found in my dad's files. "Londyn, I need to meet you in person. I found something that I think you should see." "Okay", I said without changing my tone. I'm still out of the country with Victor. I'll call you when I get back," I said and hung up the phone. Victor heard me agree to meet with Garrett once we returned back to Atlanta. This angered him that I took a business call during our trip and he pushed me into the tiny closet with his hands around my neck. With a darkness in his eyes he whispered to me, "What? You think you're more important than me?" he quietly spewed at me.

Barely able to speak with his hands tightly wrapped around my neck, I was shaking. I assured him that was not the case and I caressed his ego by saying "I'm not. You know you're like the smartest man I know. Baby stop it. I'm sorry," I begged.

He let go of my neck and I stumbled a few steps backwards almost losing my balance. I gasped for air upon his release as he stared at me with a cold look in his eyes. I had not seen that side of Victor and it scared me. He demanded to know why Garrett was calling. It made me wonder why Garrett calling me would anger him so much. Did he think there was something between me and Garrett, I questioned, or did he know something about what Garrett found? I lied to him and said that I didn't know anything. I rode back to Atlanta in silence as I was trying to figure things out about Victor. I was having second thoughts about us. He wasn't who I remembered. He was so gentle and affectionate with me in the past, but he was becoming someone I didn't even recognize.

The next day, once back in Atlanta I called Garrett, but he didn't answer my call. I resumed my normal day of attending meetings at the office and trying to figure out how my dad managed to operate all of this so easily. I was sitting at my desk combing through financial statements, trying to make sense of the manner in which the business had been operating, when Victor walked in and closed the door behind him. "Hey Sweetheart, I wanted to say I'm sorry for how I acted in Bimini." I stood up to be eye to eye with him. "I promise never to treat you like that again" he pleaded. "I want to make it up to you. Did Gus drop off the desk keys to you?" he inquired.

"Yes", I hesitantly answered.

I'm going to take you somewhere" he said grinning.

"What?" I questioned with a smile.

"Grab your purse I'm going to take you somewhere," he said boldly. Leaving the statements unattended on my desk I dashed off with Victor, eager to know what awaited me next. Holding Victor's hand, I blindly followed him. We got in his Mercedes and drove off and I tried to guess where we were going. All of my ideas were wrong as he turned towards a somewhat familiar sign, that was dirty and faded. Victor took me to the top of Arabian Mountain to a spot we use to come to and park to make-out and we would fuck in the driver's seat. So many memories of us and our sexual escapades from my youth began to emerge. As I sat there gazing out the windshield into the darkness around me I began to get aroused at the thought of having sex in the car like we did before. I wasn't sure how that was going to work because I wasn't as flexible as I once was. I took my seatbelt off and began to lean into Victor's scent, my lips grazing his ear. I dragged my lips down to his neck, his hands squeezing my thick thighs. His hands traveled up to grip my soft breasts beneath my blouse, exposing my nipples to the cool air. He turned the lights off and I began to unfasten his belt to expose his manhood. Just then, out of the darkness a man wearing all black with a black baseball hat approached the car from the passenger side and with his elbow broke the side window and reached inside the car. I was trying to fight him off and realized he was reaching for my purse resting on the dashboard. "Please don't hurt us" I yelled, terrified with tears in my eyes. Victor began to tussle with the man and then reached in the center console and pulled out a gun. "You better back the fuck up before you meet Jesus nigga!", he said to the aggressive man still gripping the strap of my purse. Victor released a single shot from the gun in the man's direction, missing him. I heard him yell "What the fuck man?", before loosening his grip on my purse and running off into the darkness.

"Are you ok my love?" Victor leaned over me, embracing my shaking body before putting the loaded gun back in the center console. I wasn't ok, I was frantic and scared. I had never heard a gunshot so close before. I could still hear the piercing bang ringing in my ears. We quickly drove off, I franticly looked around to see if I spotted the attempted robber as we drove away. We held hands the entire ride back to his house, my mind fixated on thinking about what if the night had ended differently, with someone hurt or if he had taken my purse. I was still very shaken up but at the same time I was turned on by how Victor came to my defense and grabbed his pistol to protect me. Once at Victor's house I immediately took a long hot shower to calm my nerves. After I stepped out of the shower I dried myself off with my towel and walked over to Victor who was sitting on the bed in his boxers. Then I straddled him so he could feel my warm, wet pussy on his skin until he was teased into a firm hard on and positioned himself to enter me. I buried my face into his neck, and I bounced on his lap. He pounded deep inside me and I rode him until we both exploded in pleasure.

After that night things with us seemed to improve and being with him felt better than ever. I had been calling Garrett since we got back from our trip, but I still had not been able to reach him, and no one had seen him. I wanted to know what he found, it sounded like it was important. I wondered if it had anything to do with the financial statements that disappeared from my desk the night of the attempted robbery. Victor swore he didn't know what statements I was talking about.

The next morning as I was getting ready to head into the office, I was putting finishing touches on make-up in the vanity when all of a sudden a wave of nausea overcame me, and my face felt hot. I glanced at my reflection in the vanity mirror and I looked like a ghost. All of I sudden, I felt a warmth rush over me, I leaned to my side and puked all over the rug, missing the small black trashcan by a few inches. As I wiped the chunks of breakfast from my lips I paused as I thought about the date and the fact that I'd been fucking Victor with no condom and he hadn't pulled out once since we got back together. I immediately started thinking back to the last time I had my period and realized with everything happening it was before the trip to Mexico. I called and made an appointment to see my OB/GYN. That was the day I found out I was pregnant. The emotions I felt when I heard the nurse say, "You're pregnant", were indescribable. I had never been pregnant before and I was almost forty. I wasn't careful because I didn't think I could get pregnant at my age. I really thought, if it hadn't happened by now that it would never happen.

I was feeling happy and anxious, like the fetus was about to float up through my esophagus. I couldn't stop rubbing my belly. I was stunned looking down that I then realized I was looking fuller. I hadn't paid much attention to me gaining weight since my weight was always on a seesaw. I knew it was bad luck to announce too soon but I had to tell somebody, but I wasn't sure who to tell first. I was nervous to tell

Victor. I wasn't sure how he would take the news, being that he was estranged from his two adult children. I called Angie first, I was so excited to tell her that I was going to be a mommy too. I could hear the shock in her voice, with that drawn out "Whaaat?" She was so excited and stunned by the news, especially when I told her who the father was. I thought she would hit the floor. "That's crazy Londyn. I can't believe you got back with him after all this time" she laughed, "and now you're pregnant!", she then changed her tone and yelled "I call Godmother".

"You might have to fight Joanna about that", I replied. We laughed together as we wrapped up the call and I told her I would see her soon. I hung up and called Joanna to tell her the news, but Angie had already texted her while we were talking on the phone. She was already guessing the sex of the baby, she said she felt like I was going to have a boy and she was dishing out baby names for my baby boy. I admitted to her that I hadn't told Victor yet. I just didn't know how he would react, and I was scared to tell him. After mustered up the courage I called Victor next. I told him I was planning something special for him so he should come straight home, once he left the office.

That evening I planned an intimate dinner for the two of us at his house. I told him to be home by seven that evening. I'd spent the rest of the day prepping for the meal, making sure I had every detail covered for the special news. I made his favorite meal of filet minion, grilled asparagus and sizzling sautéed truffles. After we finished dinner I asked him if he wanted dessert. After walking over and placing it in front of him I lifted the lid from the silver cake dish and revealed the double lined pregnancy test that I'd taken right before dinner. Not that I didn't trust the doctor, but I wanted to see for myself. His eyes lit up once he finally realized what he was looking at. To my surprise when I affirmed to him that I was indeed going to have his baby he was happy. He picked me up, with my feet lifted off the floor and he kissed me. He was so happy he was speechless for a moment. He put me down and he dashed into the other room, I could hear him open his desk drawer, shuffling through it. He pulled out a small white box and turned to meet me in the other room, but I was already in the doorway watching him, wondering what he was doing. To my disbelief Victor got on one knee and asked me to marry him. Inside the box was a pandora charm of a diamond ring. He unsnapped my bracelet and placed the charm on my bracelet, snapping it back in place on my tender wrist. At that moment, although there was doubt in my mind I said "Yes." I was scared of what his reaction may be if I said No. But, more so because I wanted a family and I was hopeful that things would get better with us and I was willing to try to make it work. Although excited and nervous, I allowed myself to enjoy the moment.

CHAPTER TWENTY TWO

I remember how happy I was sending out the colorful wedding announcements. I saw an invitation addressed to his son Noah Crawford. I asked him if he had spoken to his son recently. He replied, "He won't come." I know this upset Victor because he really wanted to have a relationship with his children. "What about your daughter Leah? Do you think she will come?" I asked.

"No," he demanded.

Maybe that's why he was happy about our baby, I thought. Noah and Leah didn't want anything to do with their father. Maybe he thought it was a chance for him to try his hand at fatherhood again.

Two months passed since my father's funeral and without either of his children in attendance Victor and I exchanged vows in a small ceremony at the beautiful Atlanta Botanical Gardens. I was in awe of the four-carat princess cut diamond ring that he placed on my finger. I had a flashback to Mike placing the .17 carat diamond ring on my finger inside the dark, historical courthouse in Philadelphia's City Hall. I was happy in this moment and grateful for what life was giving me. Nobody knew that I was pregnant under my flowing pearl colored wedding dress. It was somber that neither of us had our parents there, they're all deceased. I missed not having my parents there, especially my dad since I didn't allow him to walk me down the aisle the first time I got married. I wanted to make sure that I felt like he was there for this wedding. My dad would always take me to the botanical gardens in the spring, to watch the exotic flowers bloom and he always compared me to the flowers describing how each one was uniquely beautiful. I wanted to have the wedding there so I could feel him there with me.

The morning of the wedding I was so nervous, I couldn't keep anything down. Angie and Joanna stayed with me at the house with my aunt Gigi the night before the wedding. I slept in my old room, dreaming about my beginnings of passion and innocence with Victor. My aunt Gigi cornered me alone in my childhood bedroom and brought me some ginger tea to calm my stomach and she very directly asked me if I was sure that I wanted to do this. I looked at her surprised. Like how could you ask me that on my wedding day?

"I just want to make sure you are making the right decision. That man is old enough to be your father. I think your father is probably turning over in his grave today", she said.

"Don't!" I yelled, "leave my father out of this. I'm a grown woman and I know what I'm doing. I just need you to support me. That's all!", I pleaded. She looked at me with anger and disappointment in her eyes and didn't say another word. Then I noticed Aunt Gigi had something in her hand. She laid it on the bed and walked out of the room. It was my something borrowed and my something blue. On the bed were a pair of two carat sapphire earrings. The earrings were a birthday gift that my dad gave to my mom. I remember her wearing them all the time on special occasions. Part of me knew Aunt Gigi was right about my dad turning over in his grave over me marrying his colleague, but I also knew my dad would eventually support me no matter what. My friends came back to help me finalize my bridal look and then we got in the limo so I could become Mrs. Victor Crawford.

There was a young woman rippling the enchanting sounds from her harp as the ceremony began. I had chosen every colored flower and every type of flower as the wedding décor. I walked down the aisle alone, holding my bouquet. The long train to my dress covered the stepping stones in the grass as I walked towards the man of my dreams, who I prayed wouldn't turn into my nightmare. We said our vows and hopped in the white stretch limo to the reception venue. We booked the event hall at the Four Seasons for the reception dinner. My aunt Gigi was in attendance at the ceremony, but I noticed her missing from the reception. I wanted to believe she was just tired, and I knew she was still grieving the loss of my dad, so we celebrated with my friends Angie, Joanna and some of our colleagues. No one from Victor's side was in attendance. The wedding reception was elegant and fun with round tables and Chiavari chairs assembled around a square dance floor. We danced together all night to mostly classic eighties and nineties R&B. I was pregnant and got tired quickly doing my two step dance, but for a fifty-year-old man Victor could still dance and get low. After the long day we were so tired from the wedding and the reception we were too tired for sex when we got back to his house. He fell asleep in the bed still wearing his tuxedo. I had our bags packed and ready to fly out in the morning. I chose our honeymoon destination because it's a place I've always wanted to go to. It's a place my mother always talked about it for its museums, art galleries and culture.

The morning after the wedding we flew to Venice, Italy to enjoy our honeymoon together. The trip to Italy was wonderful. The weather was perfect for spring, the air was crisp, and the sunlight wrapped us in its arms. By the time we got to the hotel I was already tired. We agreed we needed a nap after we arrived at the hotel, so we would feel refreshed when we went out to dinner and explore the city later that evening. When we woke up from our nap, Victor picked out a short cocktail dress for me to wear to dinner. It wasn't what I planned to wear that night, but it wasn't worth the argument and I put on the dress he selected. Once I was dressed and freshened up with my favorite fragrance, Victor walked up to me from behind and pulled my dress up, exposing my ass cheeks. He slapped me on the ass making it sting a little as it jiggled and then he reached for my panties. I grabbed for my thong panties as I began to feel him try to force my panties down my thighs. Even though my pussy was wet because I was a little turned on by his aggression, I stopped him and reminded him that we didn't have time, or we would be late for dinner. He released me from his grip, and I put myself back together and we left the suite to make it to our reservation at Café de la Rosa. We enjoyed a delicious authentic Italian meal and we talked. I mentioned that we should by a house, and he smiled and changed the subject and began telling me how beautiful I looked. After dinner, as the night sky began to fall upon us, we walked around the elegant city admiring the beautiful architecture and the lights along the streets. We were walking along the water's edge and decided to take a private river cruise through the city. I had never done anything like that before and I was thrilled. When we were under a short bridge Victor leaned over me, pushing me back against the edge of the boat, my hands gripping the edge and he kissed my inner thigh and squeezed my ass cheeks. He licked his lips before he licked mine. My legs were anchored around his neck and I stroked his face with my clit. Before we exited on the other side of the bridge I released my excitement on his tongue. Then as the starry night light exposed us I adjusted my dress to cover my hips and I sat up right in the narrow boat, still trying to be quiet so the boat driver wouldn't hear us getting freaky in the back of the boat. I felt happy, in love and excited about my future with Victor. I felt like he was what I wanted all this time.

We spent the week in Italy and things between us felt right. We enjoyed spending time together, eating, shopping and visiting the various historical museums and galleries. When we weren't being cultured we were in the hotel room making love. He couldn't get enough of me. I enjoyed walking around the city and exploring the culture. I noticed my feet would swell quickly with all the walking we were doing. At the end of each day we would sit out on the veranda of the suite and he would rub my feet and we would just talk and share stories of my dad and his strength and his infectious laugh and discuss our future together. He wanted the baby to be a girl and he shared with me his top baby names. Life felt great and after a week of newlywed bliss I packed our bags to head home.

We announced my pregnancy after we got back from our amazing honeymoon. I was so excited about announcing my pregnancy because it was finally my turn. I sent out the baby announcements with the due date and I just let people try to figure out the math on their own. I already knew once we announced my pregnancy people would be trying to guess if I was pregnant before the wedding. Early on, my doctor said my pregnancy was considered high-risk, due to my age, and she wanted me on bed rest. I wasn't willing do to that, so I tried my best to avoid stressful situations and maintain my health, which was becoming increasingly harder to do as I got further along.

The honeymoon phase quickly wore off and Victor was becoming Dr. Jekyll and Mr. Hyde and I never knew who I was dealing with. In the beginning of my pregnancy Victor was attentive, he rubbed my back, he rubbed my feet and he called me beautiful but, as my belly grew, and I gained forty pounds I realized Victor just wanted me fat and on bed rest so he could assume the role of making decisions for the company. I refused to relinquish control. I made it a point to make sure I ate healthy and maintained my strength throughout my pregnancy. I made it a point to be at the office every day. I recognized that he didn't like me reviewing the financial statements or asking too many questions I wanted to find out why and I was determined to work until my delivery. I knew he would assume control once I went on maternity leave, but that was just temporary.

It had been months and still no one had seen Garrett. I was really concerned about this, but it didn't seem to faze Victor. One night while talking in the bedroom, I brought it up that I hadn't heard from Garrett since he called when were in Bimini. It caused an argument between us where I told him I questioned why he wasn't concerned Garrett's disappearance. He tried to convince me that Garrett had been cheating on his wife and was spending time with his side piece. I wasn't buying that story, Garrett was a good man and he loved his wife. I followed that by yelling "You're such a fucking liar!" This outburst started about Garrett and then I used the opportunity to get some other things off my chest, like how I couldn't trust him, how I hated how he tried to speak up for me, saying things I never agreed to and I brought up the comments he made about me to our colleagues insinuating that I was not able to handle the job. Maybe it was the pregnancy hormones, but I unleashed my growing frustrations on him.

Tempers were rising and we continued shouting at each other. Then my phone began to ring on the bed. I looked down and saw it was Nole and quickly sent him to voicemail before Victor could see who was calling. However, my phone ringing seemed to anger Victor even more. "So, you're cheating on me!" he shouted at me, turning this around on me. "No!" I insisted. Victor snatched my phone from my hands, I was afraid that he may look through my call log, but he threw it against the wall, smashing it into a hundred unusable pieces and then walked out of the room. I was stunned that he was behaving this way. I was angry and I stormed out of the room after him and we continued to argue. Then I really let things off my chest when I also shared with Victor that I felt like he was keeping a lot of secrets from me and I told him that I was uncomfortable living in the house that he once shared with his ex-wife. "You're mad thinking I'm cheating on you, meanwhile I'm sleeping in the same spot as your ex -wife!"

"What do you want?" he yelled.

I wasn't prepared for that question. "I want things to be better between us. I want us to buy our own house and have a fresh start, I want you to respect me, I want the Victor I once knew back", I demanded. I could tell he did not like how I was speaking to him but just then I felt a flutter in my belly. I felt the baby kicking for the first time. I grabbed Victor's hand and pressed it to my firm belly. He felt the movement and quickly pulled his hand back. He looked up at me and smiled. "I'm sorry", he begged. "If you want to buy a new house, just hire a realtor." I'm sure to Victor he saw this as an opportunity to distract me and keep me preoccupied and away from the office, but I was super excited at the idea of a new house for our growing family.

Later on, that day, I bought a new phone and I hired a realtor. I reached out to Angie and hired her as our realtor. She knew she could earn a huge commission from this sale and immediately began showing me the most gorgeous homes in Atlanta. I loved spending time with my best friend but being eight months pregnant I didn't have the energy to keep looking at houses all around the city. After what felt like a real estate tour of Atlanta Angie found us a beautiful modern home that was just what I was looking for in Sandy Springs, still not too far from Aunt Gigi. It was a little out of our discussed price range, but I showed Victor and he loved it. We didn't waste any time on making an offer and we quickly closed so we could be settled in before the baby came. Victor allowed me to take the lead on the moving arrangements. I hired Stokes & Brothers Moving Company to move us into the new house. Aunt Gigi had grown attached to Michelangelo who was getting old and sluggish so I let him stay there with her so she wouldn't be lonely. I bought all new furniture from shopping online and with Angie's assistance I organized every room of the new house except Victor's office which was off limits to everyone. I didn't want to go in there anyway, because I immediately noticed an unpleasant odor in the room. He kept the door locked and I kept Bath and Body Works plugins throughout the house to mask the seeping smell. The first room that I had complete was the nursery.

In the previous weeks Angie and Joanna had thrown me a baby shower and I was gifted everything I needed to furnish the nursery. I had her tiny clothes folded in the new white dressers and a tower of diapers and wipes in the matching changing table. I had pictures of my parents framed and hung on the pastel colored walls, because I wanted her to know her nana and pawpaw.

CHAPTER TWENTY THREE

It was towards the end of my pregnancy and I was at the point where I had a checkup with my obstetrician once a week. I called Angie and asked if she could pick me up from the new house and take me to my doctor's appointment. She was done showing houses for the day and she came to pick me up to take me to my appointment. During the appointment my doctor assured me that everything looked good and my daughter would probably be born a few weeks early. I was anxious leaving the doctor's office, the reality of going into labor soon hit me and all that anxiety made me hungry. I asked Angie to stop at a hot new restaurant, Just BBQ, so we could grab a bite to eat. The menu was some good ole Memphis barbeque. I ordered the pulled pork, mac and cheese, greens and peach cobbler and Angie ordered the pulled pork and jalapeno nachos. While we were sitting there waiting on our food I saw a familiar face walk towards us. Once the person was a few feet away from us I recognized him. It was Nole.

"Londyn is that the fine ass boy you fucked in Mexico?" Angie questioned.

"Yes", I quietly confirmed kicking her under the table.

"Hey beautiful! Why haven't you returned any of my calls?" he asked standing over me.

"Nole I don't know what to say. I've had a lot going on since my dad died."

"Oh, I'm sorry to hear that Londyn. Let me be there for you," he begged.

I leaned towards the table to cover my round belly "I'm sorry Nole, it's just not a good time for me. I'm sorry", I prayed that he would forgive me.

"She got married", Angie blurted across the table.

My head turned to Nole's reaction. I had done a good job at concealing it, but I felt like I didn't want to keep it from him any longer and I leaned back in my seat and exposed my round belly. I could tell he was hurt. "Nole, I'm sorry" I pleaded. I really didn't want to hurt him. He was so young, I didn't want to be his first heartbreak.

"I understand" he said changing his tone. "Well, congratulations", he said sounding deflated. "It was good to see you," he said and turned around and left the restaurant without the food he already paid for.

"Damn girl, you got that youngin' sprung after one night," Angie joked.

"That's not funny Angie. I don't want to hurt him," I said.

Afterwards I asked Angie to ride by Victor's house to make sure the for sale sign was up. When we pulled up I noticed an older woman standing in front of the for sale sign. When she saw me she ran to her car and sped off in a red range rover. I didn't recognize her in the quick second that I saw her face and I asked Angie if she knew who the woman was, but she did not.

Angie dropped me off at the house, on her way to get a massage. Victor wasn't home and I planned to put the finishing touches on the nursery. I wasn't due for a few more weeks, but my doctor told me not to be surprised if she came early and I wanted everything to be perfect for her arrival. I already had my hospital bag packed and by the front door,

Walking down the hallways I noticed the door to Victor's office was ajar. I pushed open the door and I noticed a file folder out on Victor's desk. Before approaching it I waddled over to the window to look out to ensure Victor's car was gone and make sure he wasn't home. I noticed an unknown car parked outside and when the driver saw me approach the window they sped off. This alarmed me, but I thought maybe Angie forgot to take the listing for this house off the market. I waddled back over to the file folder on the desk and I opened it. In that moment, a wave of intense shock surged through me, freezing my thoughts and paralyzing my movements. Everything around me blurred, leaving me dazed and discombobulated and I felt like I couldn't breathe. Inside the folder were financial records and statements of what appeared to be fake accounts. After combing through the company's financial statements, I discovered the company had been falsifying financial statements for years. I recognized some of the documents were the ones that went missing from my desk. As I flipped through the pages I discovered the company purchased the Stanford hotel some years ago and it was the most profitable real estate the company owned. As I looked closely it appeared as though each room in the hotel was organized like it's own business. I saw statements for The Laurel LLC, The Cherry LLC, The Peach LLC and so on for all the rooms. I would never forget the Laurel room since that's the room I lost my virginity in. All the money generated from the hotel was in cash which made it apparent they were running drugs and/or prostitution through the hotel. As I continued to look through the documents it appeared that most of the financial gains from Victor were due to money laundering. Then I noticed a business operating agreement for E.J. Banks Capital that was dated back ten years ago. This business operating agreement named Victor as the successor CEO. I heard a noise in the house, and I was nervous about Victor catching me in his office, but I had to keep looking. I shut the office door to hide just in case that was him. With the door closed I stood inside his office and I almost gagged due to the awful smell in the room. I continued to comb through the papers. There was also a copy of the updated business operating agreement with my name on it, as successor CEO. To my shock the new business operating agreement was dated the day my dad had the heart attack.

I wondered how much my much dad knew about the fraud. I bet this is what Garrett wanted to talk to me about, I thought. I began to feel dizzy and I felt like I was going to pass out. I felt a sharp pain in my abdomen, followed by an even more intense pain in my cervix. I felt like I needed to get to the hospital quickly. I didn't want to call Victor, so I called Aunt Gigi. She didn't answer, so I called Angie, but when she didn't answer I remembered she was getting a massage and probably had her ringer turned off, so when Angie didn't answer I called Nole.

Nole answered after two rings and said he'd just met up with his mom, but he would be right over. I texted him the address and laid on the floor amongst the boxes holding my large belly in pain. This wasn't the time for his mom to meet the cougar who took her son's virginity, but I was in no position to oppose. I was in pain and I needed help. Once they arrived Nole recognized his mother seemed confused about being at that location, then he ran in to see about me, his mother remained in the car with the engine running. "Nole, I'm so glad to see you" I admitted as he kneeled beside me to assess the severity. "I think I'm in labor I need to get to the hospital" I pleaded with pain trembling in my voice.

"Ok, where's your husband?" he asked. I didn't know where he was.

Unsure of what to do Nole said "Let me go get my mom, she's a nurse" he said standing up and racing to the door. Before he could hear me oppose he was already out of the front door. Moments later he walked in with a woman I instantly recognized although twenty years matured we both recognized each other. It hit me that I was looking at Victor's ex-wife who is Nole's mother, the same woman in the red range rover. It hit me that Noah Crawford was Nole Washington! Oh my God, I fucked Victor's son, I thought! The shock of this revelation sent me into an emotional whirlwind and my water broke. Then the pain became even more intense and was becoming excruciating. Nole still didn't understand the situation and looked confused. Then moments later Victor walked in door and saw the commotion with Nole and his ex-wife, Lisa standing over me. I was gripping my stomach lying in fetal position in a puddle of my bodily fluids, beside the open file folder. Victor looked down at me lying on the floor and he seemed more concerned about seeing the folder than he was about me being in labor on the floor, in front of his son and ex-wife.

Nole looked at Victor and shouted, "What the fuck are you doing here?", looking angry and confused.

"Motherfucker this is my house. What the fuck are you doing here?" he yelled.

"My girlfriend called me and said she needed me", he smirked looking at me attentively.

"Girlfriend?" he questioned. "Motherfucker that's my wife!" he shouted back pointing at me.

Nole stood there looking puzzled. His head swiveling back and forth between me and his father.

"This is the bitch that broke up our happy family Noah", his mother advised.

Now, Nole was looking really confused. He was trying to wrap his mind around what was happening and that his father and my abusive husband are the same person. His father was the same abusive man to me that he was to his mother. Nole's mother, began to look around at the extravagant home that he was building with his new family and she got angrier.

Lisa quietly walked out of the room and grabbed a knife from the set on top of the kitchen counter. She quickly walked back in the room with a tight grip on the knife, the blade pointed at the floor. I tried to stand up on my feet to get away, but I wasn't fast enough. With rage in her eyes she lounged the sharp blade towards me, and she stabbed the knife into my hard belly. I screamed in horror as I fell back to the floor trying not to fall on my stomach. I began losing a lot of blood from the gushing slice in my stomach and I used my hand to cover the wound. Nole ran over to me to apply pressure to the wound. His mother then looked at Victor and directed her rage towards him. She slowly walked towards him with my blood still dripping from the knife in her hand.

185

Victor backed up to the staircase and ran up the stairs and she was right behind him. I could hear his footsteps running down the hallway to get away from her. She followed him to the bedroom, and we heard them scuffle and the sound of furniture being shuffled around, until we heard a single gun shot and then silence. I was trembling, not knowing what was going on or how we were going to get out of there. I didn't want my baby to be born right there on the floor. I needed to get to the hospital, and I was afraid to know what was really happening upstairs. I begged Nole to just get me in the car and take me to the hospital. He was frantic and unsure of what to do first. He knew that I needed medical attention, but he also needed to know what was happening with his parents. "Ok, I'll get you to the hospital." He looked in my eyes with worry and fear in his eyes, "I have to go up there. I will be right back."

"No! Nole don't go up there!", I begged. Nole left my side and ran upstairs worried about his mother. He discovered a body on the bedroom floor with a single gun shot to the chest. Seconds later, I heard a struggle and then two more gun shots, and I screamed in fear as my hands covered my mouth to quiet myself. It was again eerily silent after the shots were fired. I didn't know if I was next and I couldn't stand up on my own to get away. I grabbed the file folder and crawled over to my hospital bag and stuffed it down in my hospital overnight bag that was beside me in foyer on the floor.

Moments later I looked up and saw Victor running down the stairs to come to my aid. He seemed unusually calm given the events. I asked him what happened, and he said "Don't worry about that right now. Just focus on baby girl" and he grabbed my hospital bag and carried me to the car seating me in the passenger seat, another contraction came on as he shut the car door. "Please hurry", I begged.

"I just have to grab something, and I'll be right back", he said and turned to go back in the house.

I couldn't believe him, I needed to get to the hospital and every second lost put us in danger, but I knew what he went back in the house for. He knew the police were going to comb the house and he needed to hide that file. Before he could realize the file was gone, I opened the car door holding onto the car for balance and walked around to the driver's side, as another strong contraction came on. I felt like I needed to squat but I kept my legs together and carefully got in the driver's seat and pulled out of the driveway before Victor saw me. I drove myself straight to Northside Hospital and dialed 911 to inform them of the two people with gunshot wounds at my residence.

I lived only minutes from the hospital, yet the drive felt like an eternity. I could feel my heart rate dropping and I could hear my thoughts out loud. My mind was flooded thinking about everything that was happening and every nerve in my body was electrified in pain. I was in shock that I'd slept with

Victor's son and more so, that Nole could be dead and that Victor killed him. The pain intensified, as I began to feel very warm between my thighs and I looked down to see more blood. As I was driving myself to the hospital I remember thinking that I was going to die and never see my baby. Even if I didn't make it I needed her to be ok, I thought. I looked ahead and let out a sigh of relief when I saw the hospital entrance sign. I pulled up behind an ambulance and then everything faded. Sound began to fade, my heartrate began to slow down, and my eyes began to role in the back of my head and then everything went black. I don't remember much from that point. When I reached the hospital I must've passed out from losing so much blood. I was unconscious when I was rushed through the hospital emergency lobby. I was immediately rushed into labor and delivery where by C-section Miss Victoria Jeanette Crawford graced the world at seven pounds and five ounces and twenty-one centimeters long. Hours later I woke up, opened my eyes and I screamed because I thought I was already dead. Laying in bed in the maternity room I looked down at my flattened stomach and I began to cry and panic sending my blood pressure up and setting of the alarm on the machine hooked up to my arm. The nurse rushed in and calmed me down and checked my vitals. Once I was calm I saw Victor walk into the room. I didn't know he came to the hospital. I didn't want him there. He had been in the hallway talking to two police officers who advised that he would need to come down to give a formal statement.

"Are you ready to meet your daughter?" the nurse asked me.

I shook my head so she could bring me my baby. Moments later the most adorable, brown skinned, brown eyed, chunky baby girl with a head full of curly hair was placed in my arms.

"Here she is" the nurse said adjusting the pink, white and blue cap on her head. I held my baby in my arms for the first time and felt the joy of motherhood enter my soul.

"I'll leave you all to bond" the nurse said, and she left the room.

I didn't know what to say to Victor.

"She's beautiful" Victor said to me. "She looks just like you" he continued.

I was holding my sleeping daughter in my weak arms, admiring every inch of her face. She had my mother's eyes and Victor's nose, with my smile. I noticed she had a tiny birthmark that looked like a shamrock on her chest. I stared at the birthmark with tears in my eyes.

Still troubled by the recent events I looked at Victor sternly, "Victor what happened to Garrett?" I asked him directly. Victor appeared shocked at the question.

"I don't know" he said. Victor looked in my eyes and lied to me. "Let's just enjoy the birth of our daughter and we'll deal with everything else later. Right now, nothing is more important than her."

I agreed, but I wasn't going to let it go. My aunt Gigi came to the hospital later that day with gifts to meet her great niece. She had no idea what had transpired at the new house. When Victor walked out of the room I asked Aunt Gigi to pass me my hospital bag. I reached for the file that I'd tucked inside the bag, but it wasn't there.

CHAPTER TWENTY FOUR

The next day the police came and questioned me at the hospital, but my memory was blurred from the trauma and I couldn't really remember much to answer their questions. They informed me of the two dead bodies found in my home. I had been praying that they lived, at least Nole, but I wasn't shocked to hear they both died from their gun shot wounds. Over the next few days while I recovered in the hospital, Victor was back and forth to the precinct but was never under arrest since he stated it was self-defense. After a few days we were discharged from the hospital, but we couldn't go home because the house was still a crime scene. After we shared the details of why we couldn't go home Aunt Gigi agreed to let us stay with her. I was still trying to figure out what I was going to do about Victor, and I needed to know what happened to Garrett.

As we left the hospital, I asked Victor to go by the house so we could try to pick up a few items to take to Aunt Gigi's. Everything I needed for Victoria was in the nursery. He reluctantly made the turn to head towards the new house. When we arrived at our home, there were police cars crowding the driveway. Victor looked stunned as he slammed on breaks as we approached the house. Several armed officers turned and drew their weapons at us. I was terrified, my heart was beating out of control and all I could think about was my baby in the backseat. I didn't know what was about to happen, I knew things could go left real fast. Victor looked at me with regret in his eyes and said, "I love you", then he slowly stepped out of the car. Several officers approached us, guns still pointed at him but still in our direction. Victoria began to cry but I could not reach for her or make any sudden movements, fearful that an officer may react and fire their gun, so I began to hum her favorite song *SWV's Weak,* the song I would sing to her when I was carrying her in my belly. Victoria's lungs eventually got tired and she drifted back to sleep. With the officers guns drawn they yelled for him to stop and put his hands up. Then while all the officers stood back a detective in a crisp suit walked directly up to Victor.

"Are you Victor Crawford?" the detective asked.

"Yes I am. Why?" he responded defensively.

The detective immediately responded, "You are under arrest for the murder of Garrett Stark." The detective pulled out his hand cuffs and the officers cuffed Victor's hands in front of him, while the detective read him his rights.

I was in disbelief watching all of this happening. Thankfully Victoria was still asleep in her car seat. Once placed in handcuffs he was placed in the back seat of a police car. One officer turned to me and asked if I was ok and I shook my head to say No and tears began to stream down my face. My life felt like it was attacking me from every angle and my armor was down, I felt defenseless. I'd just gotten released from the hospital and was trying to figure out life as a new mom and then my husband gets arrested and goes to jail for murder, I thought to myself. My life felt like somebody else's life, but not mine. The beginning of motherhood was not unfolding as I had envisioned. Through the tears I saw another tall man in a suit approaching me. He looked familiar from a distance. I wiped the tears away from my eyes with the napkin in the center console. As he approached me I recognized him. It was my ex-boyfriend Alex who I worked with at Philadelphia's City Hall years ago.

"Hi Londyn", he paused searching for the right words to say. "Londyn, let me say I'm sorry you're caught up in this", he said regretfully.

"Alex what is going on?", I demanded, "why are you here?"

"Londyn I'm so sorry to be the one to tell you", Alex said standing before me. "Your husband has been under investigation from the FBI for months. I work for the U.S. Attorney General and your company popped up on our radar after miscellaneous suspicious activity reports from your bank were filed. We tracked all the activity back to him and the Stanford hotel." My heart sank. "He's under investigation for money laundering, drug trafficking, prostitution and now murder. I hate to be the one to inform you of this, but after we discovered the bodies of Noah Washington and Lisa Washington we discovered another body in the home.

"What?", I shouted!

"Once the bodies were removed the detectives continued to smell the stench of death as they described it and they discovered a mummified body in the crawl space in your husband's office. It was the body of attorney Garrett Stark. Londyn I'm so sorry", Alex said standing before me, looking at my sleeping newborn in her car seat. My world disintegrated in front of me and I didn't know what to do or what to say. He continued to inform me that house would remain a crime scene and Alex offered to drive us to Aunt Gigi's because after the recent revelations I was in no shape to drive myself.

We arrived at my childhood home and Aunt Gigi came to meet us outside. She looked so concerned, as she opened her arms to me. Then she told Alex to get the baby out of the car and she walked me into the house because she said she didn't want me doing too much since I was recovering from my C-section. Alex released the car seat and carried Victoria inside placing her seat on the table. Then he got everything out of the car and brought it inside the house.

Once inside the house I sat down on the couch with Victoria still asleep in her car seat, resting on top of the coffee table. Alex sat beside me, admiring my face and held my hand. Londyn I know this is not the best time to reconnect with you, but if you need anything please reach out to me. My phone number is the same", he affirmed.

"Thank you", I said forcing a smile. "Thanks for looking out for me."

"Of course," he said embracing me.

"Alex I just need you to do one thing for me", I said pulling away from his embrace. "Make sure he doesn't get out."

"I don't think he'll ever get out", he said and then he left.

Once Alex was gone I sat there thinking about everything that was happening. I couldn't handle any more surprises. I was trying to process everything without giving myself the biggest aneurysm. I never thought so much could be put on me at one time and I didn't know how I was going to get through it but that little chubby beautiful baby girl needed me to quickly figure it out.

Later on, that night Angie and Joanna came over to see the baby and comfort me in light of the recent life events. They were as shocked as I was to learn of all the drama surrounding Nole being Victor's son.

Despite the devastating loss of Nole and my husband's arrest, I was determined to pick up the pieces of my shattered life and move forward. As the news of my husband's arrest spread, I found comfort in the support of my close friends and family, who stood by my side through the horrifying ordeal.

In the days following the arrest Alex communicated with me daily, calling and texting to see about me and baby girl. He came by to see me and update me on the case almost daily. For someone who never wanted children he was very fond of Victoria and her eyes seemed to light up when she saw him.

After a few months the trial began and with all the evidence against him the trial quickly ended in a guilty verdict resulting in three consecutive life sentences for the murders plus another twenty years for money laundering, prostitution and other financial crimes. Once the trial was over I thanked Alex for everything he did to make sure Victor was brought to justice. He asked me if once things settled I would consider going out with him. I was in no shape to start dating, "As you can see my view on family hasn't changed", I said adjusting Victoria in my arms. "Now I come as a package deal with a child, so I'm sure I can't entertain you."

"I understand", he said. "Just remember people change." He kissed me on the cheek and left me standing there speechless with Victoria in my arms. Throughout the trial Alex was very supportive and kept me informed. He was relentlessly building his case against Victor to ensure he spent the rest of his life behind bars

After the emotional trial I needed to check out for a few days. I had been doing an unbalanced job of being a mother and CEO. I was more mother than CEO at this time and a personal life was nonexistent. I had been bringing Victoria to the office with me and still staying with Aunt Gigi until I could sell the house and find us a new home. I could never go back in that house with the sound of death ringing in my ears and the smell of rotting corpse in the air.

 After taking my time to mentally deal with all that had happened and adapt to motherhood I decided to take a quick trip. I arranged for a private jet to take myself, Victoria and my mother's ashes to London, England. I felt proud that I could finally honor my mother by bringing her to the place she always dreamed of. My mother would have loved it there. The art, the music, the food was all so elegant. A part of me felt my mother's presence the moment we stepped into cool London air.

 Victoria was only a few months old, but I wanted her to see everything, even knowing she wouldn't remember it. I had something special planned for the next day.

 We woke up the next morning, early as usual and I dressed us in matching dresses for what I had planned. I chose the perfect sunny day, the sun rays absorbed into my glowing skin. Pushing the stroller carrying both my daughter and my mother we stood on top of London Bridge. I shared with my baby girl why this was so significant showing her the urn that held my mother's remains. I then opened the urn with tears in my eyes and I released my mother's ashes along London Bridge. After that symbolic gesture I spent the rest of the day sightseeing and enjoying the native pastries with my daughter. It was a cleansing trip and I was ready to begin my new normal with a refreshed mind. The next day we got back on the plane to go home to Atlanta.

I was putting Victoria to sleep in her crib beside my bed in my childhood bedroom when I saw the message. It was a text from Alex. I didn't hesitate to open it. It read.

Londyn I don't know where to begin. There's so much I want to say to you. I want to hear your voice. Call me.

I read the message over and over again. He broke my heart once and I didn't want to give him the chance to do it again, but my vulnerability made me call him anyway. I wasn't expecting him to pick up so quickly. He sounded excited and surprised to hear my voice on the phone. "Thanks for calling. I didn't expect you to call so soon," he chuckled. I rolled my eyes into the phone. "No seriously," he said clearing his voice, "I'm so glad to have you back in my life. I was a fool when we dated years ago. I didn't realize what I had in a woman like you. I can't believe I let you go." He paused hesitantly making his next statement. "The truth is I knew you wanted children more than anything and I knew I couldn't give them to you. So, I didn't fight it when you ended things with us. I was embarrassed to tell you that I'm unable to get a woman pregnant due to an injury to my testicles when I was younger." I was definitely shocked at that confession, I wish he would have just told me that when we were together before. "Victoria is almost as beautiful as her mother", he declared "I adore her, and I would love a second chance with you, to be there for both of you. I promise not to fumble you this time", he begged.

I told him that I was open to seeing him again, but I wanted to take things slow. I had so much on my plate, and I needed to focus my attention on my daughter and on my work.

Alex was patient with me. I gradually found healing and happiness in my personal life. I surrounded myself with my friends who had become my chosen family. They provided the support and love I needed to continue moving forward.

Eventually, I also allowed myself to explore a new relationship with Alex, cautiously opening my heart to the possibility of love once again. He embraced my scars and supported my dreams. Together, we embarked on a journey of love, growth, and mutual support. Our personal and professional lives began to blend harmoniously, as Alex also shared in my passion for building and supporting underserved communities and he eventually ran for public office. We became a power couple, inspiring others with our shared values and commitment to making a difference.

As I looked back on my incredible experiences, I realized that sometimes life's most painful chapters may lead to the most extraordinary transformations. Through the ashes of heartbreak, loss and timeless temptations, I reclaimed my own happiness.

Thank You from the Author

I wanted to take a moment to express my sincerest gratitude for you choosing to read my book, Timeless Temptation an erotic novel. It means the world to me, and I am truly honored to have had the opportunity to share my words and thoughts with you.

Your willingness to invest your time and immerse yourself in the world I've created is a gift I truly appreciate.

As an author, there is no greater reward than knowing that my words have resonated with readers like you. I'm humbly grateful.

Thank you

Shawna Michelle

Follow me on Instagram:

shawnamichelleatl

Please leave a review on Amazon at amazon.com/author/shawnamichelle or on Runwayvixxen.com

TIMELESS TEMPTATION An erotic drama

www.ingramcontent.com/pod-product-compliance
Lightning Source LLC
Chambersburg PA
CBHW050400030726
47503CB00006B/1955